"Wake up, sleepyhead," Neil whispered.

Ginnie peered suspiciously at her husband. "Don't you have to go to the office? Or have a meeting with the election committee?"

"No to both."

She couldn't believe it! There hadn't been a Saturday in months when he hadn't run off. "Then why did you set the alarm?"

"It might seem unromantic, but with our busy schedules, I wanted to make sure we have plenty of time for this. Kiss me, Ginnie."

It was all the invitation she needed. She slid her arms around him and met his embrace. As absorbed as she was, she barely heard the click of the bedroom door.

But when Neil muttered an oath, she knew that Todd was standing there. "Gee, Dad. I'm sorry," he said.

But Ginnie heard no sorrow in those words. She hoped it was her imagination, but what she heard was a sneaky pleasure in having interrupted them....

Dear Reader,

There's a nip in the air, now that fall is here, so why not curl up with a good book to keep warm? We've got six of them this month, right here in Silhouette Intimate Moments. Take Modean Moon's *From This Day Forward,* for example. This Intimate Moments Extra title is a deeply emotional look at the break-up—and makeup—of a marriage. Your heart will ache along with heroine Ginnie Kendrick's when she thinks she's lost Neil forever, and your heart will soar along with hers, too, when at last she gets him back again.

The rest of the month is terrific, too. Jo Leigh is back with *Everyday Hero.* Who can resist a bad boy like T. J. Russo? Not Kate Dugan, that's for sure! Then there's Linda Randall Wisdom's *No More Mister Nice Guy.* Jed Hawkins is definitely tough, but even a tough guy has a heart—as Shelby Carlisle can testify by the end of this compelling novel. Suzanne Brockmann's TALL, DARK AND DANGEROUS miniseries continues with *Forever Blue,* about Lucy Tait and Blue McCoy, a hero as true blue as his name. Welcome Audra Adams to the line with *Mommy's Hero,* and watch as the world's cutest twin girls win over the recluse next door. Okay, their mom has something to do with his change of heart, too. Finally, greet our newest author, Roberta Tobeck. She's part of our WOMEN TO WATCH new author promotion, and once you've read *Under Cover of the Night,* you'll know why we're so keen on her.

Enjoy—and come back next month for six more top-notch novels of romance the Intimate Moments way.

Leslie Wainger

Leslie Wainger,
Senior Editor and Editorial Coordinator

Please address questions and book requests to:
Silhouette Reader Service
U.S.: 3010 Walden Ave., P.O. Box 1325, Buffalo, NY 14269
Canadian: P.O. Box 609, Fort Erie, Ont. L2A 5X3

FROM THIS DAY FORWARD

MODEAN MOON

Silhouette®

INTIMATE™MOMENTS®

Published by Silhouette Books

America's Publisher of Contemporary Romance

 SILHOUETTE BOOKS

ISBN 0-373-07739-4

FROM THIS DAY FORWARD

Printed in U.S.A.

Books by Modean Moon

Silhouette Intimate Moments

From This Day Forward #739

Silhouette Desire

The Giving #868
Interrupted Honeymoon #904
Forgotten Vows #995

MODEAN MOON

once believed she could do anything she wanted. Now she realizes there is not enough time in one life to do everything. As a result, she says her writing is a means of exploring paths not taken. Currently she works as a land title researcher, determining land or mineral ownership for clients. Modean lives in Oklahoma on a hill overlooking a small town. She shares a restored Victorian farmhouse with a six-pound dog, a twelve-pound cat and, reportedly, a resident ghost.

Chapter 1

The ringing of the telephone didn't alarm Ginnie. Why should it? It had rung repeatedly all evening as her friends called with season's wishes and last-minute revisions in holiday plans. She barely heard it over the recorded music-box Christmas carols and the laughter of her best friend Cassie's three sons, roughhousing on the floor with their present to her, a ten-week-old collie pup.

She did hear it, though, and handed the armload of coats to Cassie. "It's probably Frank." She grinned and paused long enough to pluck a handmade ceramic ornament from the carpet and hang it high on the tree before stepping around opened toys and piles of discarded ribbon and paper. "I'll bet he's worried about what's keeping us."

She was still grinning as she picked up the receiver, more interested in Cassie's attempts to get the boys into their coats and away from the dog than she was, at the moment, in the call.

"Hello." Her voice carried her laughter.

"Will you accept the charges on a collect call from Todd Kendrick?"

Ginnie's hand clenched on the receiver and she stood stunned into silence, unaware of anything, not even the feeling of her nails digging into her palm. One by one, sensations returned to her—the pleasant mingled scents of bayberry and fresh fir, the glow of the dying fire, the giggles of the boys and Cassie's frustrated coaxing.

No! The word roared through her, then whimpered in her mind as her thoughts darted without coherence, as fleeting and random as the tiny lights on the tree across the room. *Why now?* Where is he? Oh, God, what can I do? Can I just hang up? *What does he want?*

"Ma'am?" the operator repeated more distinctly. "Will you accept—"

"Yes," Ginnie said quietly, acknowledging that something far beyond her control had been set in motion, knowing that she had no choice but to talk to him.

"Ginnie?" His voice was deeper, no longer the childish one she remembered. "Mom?"

Mom. After all those years of waiting, and praying, now he'd finally said it. She stood quite still, consciously not allowing herself to show any weakness by slumping. "Yes, Todd?" Her voice was barely audible. It was the best she could do. Her heart pounded against her breastbone, its sounds competing with those coming over the faintly crackling line. "What do you want?"

"I'm coming home for Christmas," he announced triumphantly.

It was a joke. It had to be a joke. Didn't he know what torture he was putting her through? Or did he know and was he doing it deliberately?

She put one hand against the wall for support. "Where are you?"

"Oh." He paused for a second. "I don't know. Some pay phone just off the highway. It's awful cold out here. Tell Dad I'm going to be a little late, because I'm having trouble getting rides."

Pay phone? Highway? "Todd?" *Tell Dad?* "Todd." She fought down the urge to yell at him. "Your father and I—you do remember that your father and I—"

"Sure," he said. "Do you still have the Christmas tree in front of the big bay window? I love it over there."

"Todd? Todd, your father and I—" She had no idea of how to reason with him. "We don't live on the farm anymore."

"Oh, gee. That's too bad. Don't worry. I'll find you."

"Todd." She knew she was going to scream any moment now. "Where are you?"

"Ginnie." He lowered his voice and ignored her question. "I haven't forgotten."

She bit down hard on her lower lip. No. He wouldn't have forgotten. He had sworn not to.

"See you," he promised. "Soon."

Too late she remembered the operator who had connected the call. Too late she clicked down on the buttons, trying to summon her, trying to find out where the call had been placed. She continued clicking them long after the dial tone announced an open line.

"Ginnie?"

Cassie stood in the doorway with Ginnie's coat draped over her arm as she studied her intently. "What's wrong? There hasn't been an accident, has there?"

An accident? Vaguely Ginnie remembered the snow that had so uncharacteristically begun drifting down late that afternoon, powdering the trees, the lawns and the streets.

"No," she said, attempting to reassure her friend. "No accident."

She saw by Cassie's still-worried expression that her attempt hadn't worked.

"Then what... You look just awful, Ginnie. What was that phone call about?"

Ginnie shook her head slowly, as if in denying Cassie's question, she could deny all that had just happened. "It's probably nothing," she told her, "but I have to make some calls."

She glanced at the slim watch on her wrist. "It's almost eleven thirty. The choir will be starting soon. If you don't get a move on, you'll miss Frank's solo."

"What about you? Aren't you coming to Mass?"

"Yes... No..."

"I don't know? Maybe?" Cassie finished for her as Ginnie tried to find an answer.

"Maybe," Ginnie said. "Now, go on." She smiled, knowing that Cassie still wasn't reassured. "If I can get the answers I need, I'll be there. If not—if not, I'll try to explain tomorrow at dinner."

She kept her smile firmly in place until she saw Cassie and the boys safely in the car. It slid from her as she collapsed against the door, twisting the dead-bolt lock and leaning her head against the door facing. She took a shuddering breath and pushed away from the door. *I will be calm,* she told herself as she walked mechanically through the house, checking the locks on all the doors and windows and turning on the pitifully few outside lights.

I won't panic, she insisted, but her fingers fumbled on the pages of her address book. She would simply ask for information. Nothing else. She wouldn't ask him for help, and she wouldn't be disappointed or vindictive when he didn't offer any.

She had only the number for his Little Rock law office. Somewhere in her papers was the card on which she had written his unlisted home number, but she had no idea where. She counted each ring until, on the fifth, an impersonal female voice answered. Good. He still kept his answering service.

"I need to talk to Neil Kendrick." Good. Her voice didn't break.

"I'll be happy to take a message, but Mr. Kendrick won't be back in the office until the twenty-sixth."

"I realize that." Ginnie spoke evenly, knowing she didn't dare relax her tenuous control, not even in her voice. "But I also know that he has given you a number where he can be reached in an emergency. Please call him and tell him to get in touch with Virginia Kendrick, immediately, concerning an urgent family matter." Good. She'd managed to make it sound like a calm, competent request.

"Oh."

Ginnie could sense the operator's curiosity, but she remained silent, waiting.

"Yes, I do have a number Ms.—Mrs.? Kendrick. But—you did say that it's urgent?"

In spite of her own anxiety, Ginnie felt a smile quirk her lips. At one time, Neil's temper had been the topic of discussions from Fort Smith to Memphis, but she doubted that this woman would ever see anything but his charm.

"Urgent," she repeated softly.

"All right," the operator said, sounding as though she were only half-convinced but had decided to go ahead. "I'll call him."

"Thank you." Good. Now all she had to do was wait the few minutes until Neil returned her call. Being calm and rational wasn't all that difficult. Not if she set her mind to it. Not if she stayed busy. She could stay busy a few minutes.

She gathered discarded wrapping paper and put it in the trash. She put another log on the fire. She stacked the opened packages under the tree. She set her alarm clock for the following morning. She rechecked the front-door lock. She even added water to the base of the tree, and while doing so she found one unopened package.

"Oh." She rocked back on her heels and stared at it numbly. "Frank's sweater," she murmured. "Cassie forgot to take it."

The telephone rang, and she forgot Frank's sweater as she scrambled to her feet.

"What is it, Ginnie?" Neil's rich, assured voice floated to her over a backdrop of music and laughter, telling her that he was at a party, probably having as good a time as she had been having before her own unexpected phone call. And she had interrupted him. She could imagine the irritation that he masked.

"What is it, Ginnie?" he repeated. "It's been too long for this to be holiday nostalgia, so it has to be something you consider important."

Years of hearing censure in everything he said to her had conditioned her well. So he was upset with her for disturbing his plans? She was going though hell, and *he* was upset? In an instant, her resolve to be calm and rational deserted her.

"Damn you, Neil Kendrick. You promised you'd tell me if they ever let him out."

Silence crackled through the line before she once again heard his voice as she had heard it too many times in the past. Patient. Resigned. "What are you talking about?"

"Todd!" she cried. "You promised you'd tell me if they ever let him out."

"And I will."

"When? After he comes knocking on my door?"

"Ginnie, I saw him this morning. By now he ought to be sound asleep. In his bed. At the sanitarium—"

"Well, if he is," she interrupted, "how did he get to a pay phone, God knows where, to call me and tell me he is hitchhiking home for Christmas?"

Neil's voice cut through her rising hysteria. "Tell me exactly what he said."

Damn! He didn't know. He hadn't told her because he didn't know. Maybe—maybe Todd wasn't looking for her. As coherently as she could, Ginnie repeated the conversation.

"I'll call you right back." Neil spoke quickly, and his clipped words told her he wanted no argument at this time. "Lock your doors."

Once again she was left holding a dial tone to her ear. She replaced the receiver and looked around the room. Neil was probably right. She heard herself laugh helplessly. Todd was probably at the sanitarium. By now, he might even be asleep. And there was one more wedge between her and Neil, driven there by herself. As though one more could possibly make things worse. But why had she yelled at him? Hadn't the divorce and time healed anything? Why did he still have the power to set her off like that?

She checked the lock on the back door and began loading eggnog cups into the dishwasher. Neil was right. Todd was there. Asleep by now. But on the first shrill ring of the telephone, the cup in her hand slipped free and shattered against the sink.

"Yes?"

"Ginnie, there's probably no reason to worry—"

He wasn't there! "Where is he?"

"He's usually not violent."

"Where is he?"

She heard Neil sigh. No background noises intruded now. Had he moved to another room? Or had his party ended as abruptly as hers had?

"They don't know. He was in bed at nine but he's not there now. They're notifying the local authorities."

"Three hours," she whispered. "And they didn't know?"

"He's—hold on." She heard a muffled sound through the line and then Neil's voice, distant, talking to someone in the room with him. "I don't know yet. I'll be out in a minute."

"I'm sorry for the interruption," he said to her. "Todd has walked away a couple of times. He's always come back. But he's never left at night before."

Ginnie looked around the old-fashioned kitchen with its gay red gingham curtains. The bright red telephone in her hand mocked her. She'd always felt so safe here.

"Do you mean that he's been able to leave when he wanted . . . all this time?"

"No! No," Neil said more softly. "It's just that he's been . . . well-behaved, lately. When he's that way, they relax some of his restrictions."

"And he repays that trust by walking away?"

"Ginnie, I know you're afraid. Do you have anyone with you?"

"No."

"Do you have anyone you can call, or anyplace you can go?"

"And hide?" she asked. "Just waiting for him to find me?"

"Listen carefully. Calm down and listen carefully. I know we all agreed that it would be better if you didn't visit Todd, but if you had, you might not be so frightened. Todd—Todd gets lost in time. Sometimes just for minutes, but sometimes for days. And when he's . . . lost, he's reliving something that happened, maybe years ago, maybe only in a fantasy. If he does come to you, find out where he is. In his head, he may be only twelve years old, coming home for Christmas."

She held the phone to her cheek a long time before she could speak. "But he may be sixteen?"

She heard Neil's voice break then. "Yes. He may be sixteen." For just a moment he sounded as defeated as she felt. "Have you called the police department yet?"

"No."

"I'll call them for you. Then I have to run by my apartment. But I'll get to your place as soon as I can."

Had she even hoped he'd do that? She couldn't tell, now. "You're coming here?"

"Of course." His voice was lower, comforting her across the miles and the years that separated them.

"But it's—it's Christmas," she stammered.

"I know."

"And it's—it's—"

"It's what, Ginnie?" he asked softly.

"It's—" It was what? Unexpected? That went without saying. Devastating? That he would drive through the night to be with her? Not her, she reminded herself. His son. Necessary, she realized as she felt tears sliding down her cheeks. Oh, so necessary. "It's snowing," she said, trying to stop her tears, wanting to keep any knowledge of them from Neil, and knowing she hadn't.

"Then the drive may take a little longer. Will you be all right?"

She nodded and then realized the telephone line couldn't carry that answer. "Yes."

Ginnie heard the church bells a few minutes later. It was midnight, only midnight, and she felt as though the night had gone on forever. It would have before Neil could get here, she thought. She clicked off his schedule in her mind. Pleasant Gap was an hour and a half north of Little Rock, in the daylight, on dry roads. The mountains would be treacherous tonight. And he still had to make telephone calls. And say his goodbyes. And go by his apartment. It was going to be a long night.

She struck a match, lit a burner on the antique Roper range, filled her red kettle and stood for min-

utes trying to decide between tea and hot chocolate.
When the kettle whistled, demanding a decision, she
still hadn't decided. She turned off the burner and
went into the living room.

A very long night, indeed.

The puppy whimpered in his sleep, a log popped in
the fireplace and outside a branch scraped against a
window screen, but all else was silent. Oppressively
silent.

She turned on the stereo and set it to play repeatedly. The tinkling music-box sounds seemed, now, in-
appropriate, and yet they filled the corners of the
room and the shadowy recesses of her mind. They
filled them innocuously, true, and perhaps they
couldn't drive out any large demons, but the little
ones, the ones that were lurking about ready to make
mischief, would find those spaces filled and have to
move on.

Ginnie parted the sheer curtains and looked out into
the now fiercely swirling snow. On the street below,
barely visible, a police car crept past, the light from its
spotlight refracted into thousands of tiny crystals as it
tried to scan the ancient and overgrown privet hedge
that guarded her boundary lines. So. He had done
that. He had called them. That was one thing less he
had to do. Was he on his way yet?

She settled down on the floor beside the coffee table, tucked her feet under her long wool skirt and
leaned back against the couch, staring into the fire.

She had sat that way for countless evenings, enjoy-
ing her solitude, but now the isolation bore in on her,
reminding her of how alone she really was, while out
in the night Todd made his way to her.

How had it started? When could they have done something about it?

Ginnie glanced at the tree. The first Christmas. The Christmas when she was so full of being a new wife and a new mother. Todd was twelve. Was he ever really only twelve? Although small for his age, he had always seemed so much older. They had bought a tree that year. Living in Little Rock, they had no way to cut one. Todd had helped decorate the tree. She'd taken one special ornament from the box and explained to him that it had been on every tree she'd ever had. He'd reached for it and she'd let him hold it a moment before she took it and hung it among the pine needles. It was the last ornament to be placed, and she and Todd had stood back to admire their handiwork. Neil had come to stand beside them, put his arm around her and hugged her close. She'd turned into his embrace, full of love for him, and met his light kiss eagerly. The next day, she'd noticed a small cut on Todd's finger, and days later, when taking down the tree, she'd found what was left of her special ornament.

Had that been the first sign? "You have a memory that just won't quit," Neil had said to her—no, had yelled at her later, much later, just before the final fight. "You never forget anything. But do you ever understand the significance of it?"

Maybe he was right; maybe she didn't understand, she thought, resting her forehead on her knees, but her memory served her well in spite of that. If she worked at it, she could remember all the bad times, concentrating on them and relegating the good times to a deep dark closet to be taken out only when the pain was bearable.

She caught a glimpse of something shiny peeping out from under the edge of the couch and reached idly for it, finding a Polaroid snapshot, one of many they had taken that evening, one that must have been misplaced in the excitement. It showed her, on the floor with Paul, Cassie and Frank's youngest, laughing as he tied a big red bow around the wriggling puppy.

She leaned closer to the soft pool of light from the floor lamp and examined the picture and the stranger she saw in it. The emerald-green wool draped gracefully over her small figure. Its color matched that of her eyes and complemented the warm honey blond of her hair, caught now in a loose knot atop her head, but with its soft curls as willful and unrestrainable as ever. The cowl collar of her dress was a perfect foil for a long slender neck and a delicate, almost fragile jaw and high cheekbones. She still looked helplessly young, she thought ruefully. If nothing else, the past few years should have given her at least the appearance of maturity. Even now she was sometimes mistaken for one of her journalism students. Maybe it was the slight tilt to an otherwise straight and classic nose. Maybe it was the hint of fullness in her lower lip. But in this picture, she *was* pretty.

What a strange thing to discover at thirty.

Neil had told her that she was beautiful, often, at first, but she had never quite believed him. She'd never doubted that she was attractive. But beautiful? No. She'd always thought herself too—too young-looking, too short, too thin, too underendowed. Cute, perhaps. Not beautiful. Could he have been right about that, too?

She was in her bedroom before she realized why she'd gone there, moving an enormous flowering white African violet from the top of a big square trunk.

"Don't do this to yourself," she whispered urgently, but she knew that she would.

Inside the trunk, under piles of blankets, rested a shallow wooden box, and inside that box she had buried the tangible evidence of her marriage. She lifted the box from its burrow and carried it into the living room. She curled on the corner of the couch, pulled the floor lamp closer to her, touched the top of the box hesitantly and opened it.

Chapter 2

It was all there—divorce decree, marriage license, wedding ring and pictures. Hopes and disappointments. Laughter and loss. Ginnie hadn't allowed herself to look at any of it for almost two years. Not since...

Todd's middle-school picture, the latest she had of him, was what she had studied then. She put the documents and ring box on the seat beside her and pulled the picture from the top of the stack. He had been such a beautiful child, the image of his father and his grandfather. Three generations of Kendrick men stared back at her from dark brown eyes beneath thick, rich eyebrows. A shock of coffee-brown hair had rejected the photographer's orders and swept defiantly over his broad forehead. His eyes gleamed with anticipation, and a careless smile parted his lips to expose perfect white teeth and emphasize the dimple in his chin, which, when maturity firmed his already strong jaw, would be a cleft. She hadn't found an answer two years ago. No matter how hard she looked, she knew she wouldn't find one now.

She felt the pressure of still more tears behind her eyes and the twist of a grief she had thought was long ago dealt with.

It was a trick of the light. She knew it had to be. But now Todd's eyes were glittering with rage, an unspeakable, unanswerable anger, directed at her. She turned the picture facedown on the cushion, and as if that wasn't enough, she slid it under the pile of documents and held her hand over it until she could slow her racing heart and silence the voices her imagination was all too ready to provide.

Was there an answer? She shook her head in defiance of the tears that threatened to spill over. Or was it all just some horrible, pointless waste?

Reluctantly, Ginnie reached for the picture at the bottom of the box, also a Polaroid snapshot, this one taken by an unknown tourist who had walked up to them, almost apologetically, as she and Neil sat on the seawall in Galveston and offered to take a photo of them if they would just take one of him and his son. God, how she had loved Neil. No one looking at the poorly composed photograph would ever doubt that. She stifled a laugh. Looking at him, one would swear he loved her, too. She'd thought he did. But that was before the doubts began creeping in. That was when she was still wrapped in the wonder and the excitement, the magic of having been singled out by him. He'd noticed her when she was a member of the press corps covering what was now recognized as a landmark case in Arkansas law. He was a charismatic and triumphant young attorney who, in a ten-day trial, had alternately chipped and then bulldozed through the state's reportedly airtight case, gaining an acquittal for his client and cementing for himself the reputation of being *the* criminal attorney.

She didn't remember the questions she'd asked, but she did remember the way Neil's eyes acknowledged those questions, and she did remember the easy grace with which he'd fielded questions from the other reporters and how, after he signaled the end of the press conference, he'd spoken her name almost questioningly. Surprised, she turned back to him and found his warm, engaging smile all for her.

"I don't suppose you could...I mean... Damn it!" he'd said.

She stared at him, wide eyed and wondering. The man who had just proven his eloquence before hundreds of people was actually having trouble speaking.

She quirked an eyebrow, smiled hesitantly and waited.

He grinned, an apologetic, lopsided grin, and Ginnie knew at that instant she was lost forever.

"What I'm trying to say is that if your schedule would permit..."

"Yes?" she asked, hating her inability to hide her breathless anticipation.

"Will you have dinner with me?" he asked abruptly.

She nodded. Something as simple as forming words seemed suddenly beyond her power.

It was hard, now, to remember that he had ever been speechless. She had tried, for a while, to hold on to that one sign of vulnerability, that one evidence of humanity in him, until she had been forced to relegate it to the shallow wooden casket with her other painful treasures.

Neil had found his voice that night. Over dinner. Keyed to a fine pitch by the intensity of the ten days of trial, he'd talked, and talked, and talked. And she'd listened, dazed and intrigued, and totally captivated, until she sensed he was winding down, ready to surrender to the exhaustion she knew awaited him. Then she'd excused herself, returned to her desk, wrote her story, went home and tried to sleep.

Neil's phone call caught her the next afternoon as she was leaving the office.

"Ginnie." His voice caressed her. "I have to see you again."

This time her powers of speech were a little better. "Oh, yes."

A month later, after seeing him every night, working every day, and sleeping, well, practically not at all, she again met Neil at the courthouse. They went before a judge, a friend of Neil's. Ginnie's roommate was her maid of honor. Neil's partner, Kirk Williams, was his best man. Their only guest was Neil's son, Todd, then twelve and ill-at-ease in his new blue suit, watching, carefully watching each event of his father's wedding and not at all happy when, after a brief celebratory dinner, he was sent home with Kirk.

Maybe they should have talked more about Todd before the wedding, but Ginnie knew it would have made no difference. She would have married Neil had he had six children. One beautiful, silent boy couldn't have stopped her. Then.

Oh, be honest with yourself, Ginnie, she raged silently. Was it Todd who drove the first wedge between you and Neil? Or was it something within Neil?

Or did you do it yourself?

Tea, she decided suddenly. She would have tea. She would sit in the brightness of her kitchen and drink hot tea and not think of Neil—that was over—or Todd. A shudder ran through her. Would that ever be over?

She left the living room and walked into the kitchen. Needles of snow pelted against the windows and piled even higher in their corners as Ginnie lit the stove and waited for the water to heat again. The outside light illuminated only the whiteness, no details, of the backyard. When the kettle's whistle pierced the silence, she filled her cup and set the kettle on the warming ledge. She lit all the burners and remained at the stove, chafing her arms, waiting for the fire to take the chill from the room.

Warm. It had been warm in Galveston. She leaned against the oven, still hugging herself, as a wave of longing swept through her. She threw her head back and sighed. She had been so young, much younger than she should have been at twenty-four, much too naive to suspect that Neil's careful and oh, so, wonderful lovemaking had been anything other than an expression of a love as deep and consuming as hers.

She had learned slowly, refusing to harbor the doubts that crept in on her until forced to, refusing to accept that Neil's work did not really require the hours he gave it, refusing to acknowledge that his political ambitions did require that he present at least the facade of a happy marriage, refusing to recognize that he had needed a mother for his son—a son who wanted no one between himself and his father.

Her hands on her arms were too reminiscent of Neil's hands. Her self-hug, though innocently started, was too reminiscent of his embraces. She balled her hands into fists and beat impotently against the white porcelain of the oven wall behind her.

"Remember the bad times," she moaned. "Remember the bad times. Remember the bad times!"

But now she couldn't. Now all she could remember was the salty taste of his skin and the comfort of his arms holding her close. The hotel where they'd stayed on their honeymoon jutted out over the gulf. In the distance, a storm was building, darkening the sky and roiling the clouds, and the gulf waters were beginning to peak and break, but inside there was only the quiet hum of the air-conditioning and the mingled sounds of their steadying breathing. They were alone in the world, just the two of them, wrapped in a cocoon of contentment.

Neil cupped her face with his hand and traced her cheek with his thumb.

"I love you, Ginnie. I never thought I'd be able to say those words again. I never thought I'd know what they really mean."

She turned in his arms, sure of his love, sure of their future. Her lips found the soft velvet of his skin just above his heart and with the tip of her tongue she traced the outline of her mouth against his chest. She could feel his heart beating and drew a deep breath as it quickened at her touch.

"I love you, Ginnie." She felt the words as he whispered them into the rapidly darkening room. "And Todd will, too."

She willed herself to relax as her muscles began tightening. He was only answering the question she had not yet dared to ask.

"I hope so," she murmured against his chest.

He tightened his arm around her. "Trust me. It won't be long."

"Should we have waited, Neil? Should we have given him more time to adjust to me, to adjust to the idea—"

"Ssh." He brushed a strand of hair from her cheek. "Todd needs you. Almost as much as I do. He just doesn't realize it yet."

He would realize it. She accepted Neil's words. Too many wonderful things were unfolding for her to worry, needlessly. She'd held the thought, though, and by the time they returned to Little Rock, it was a part of her. Unfortunately, it had not been a part of Todd.

Ginnie recognized Todd's minor rebellions as an attempt to irritate her, make her lose her temper and show herself in a bad light to Neil. She recognized it and refused to be drawn into a power play with a twelve-year-old. And it wasn't a constant struggle. So many things about Todd reached out to her—his fierce independence, his gentle care of Charlie, the old, blind collie that slept beside his bed. He was a bright and loving boy when he chose to be, but he seldom chose to be when he and Ginnie were alone.

Their first night home had set the pattern. She and Neil had picked Todd up on their return to town and taken him to dinner, to an out-of-the-way seafood place down on the river. Todd had monopolized his father's attention, excluding Ginnie from the conversation. She'd let him. After all, she had had Neil's undivided attention for ten glorious days. She understood Todd's need.

That evening, when Todd came into the den to say good-night, even at twelve, he went willingly to his father for a hug.

"Say good-night to Ginnie," Neil prompted.

Ginnie bent to embrace the boy, but he backed away from her. "You're not my mother," he said quietly.

She let her arms drop to her sides and watched him walk stiffly from the room.

"Ginnie?" Neil rose from his chair and came to stand beside her. "I'm sorry. I'll speak to him."

"No." She smiled, trying to hide the hurt Todd's snub had caused. "That might make matters worse. I guess..." She drew a deep breath, only beginning to realize the magnitude of the job facing her. "I guess I'm going to have to work harder at this than I thought."

Later that evening, she had begun learning how much harder she was going to have to work. Returning to the den after her bath, she heard a low voice in Todd's room. Hesitantly, not wanting to intrude, she paused at the door. There was only the one voice, Todd's, speaking softly and insistently. Curious, she pushed open the door and in the shaft of light from the hallway, she saw him curled on the floor, his head resting on Charlie's side. He looked up guiltily. She smiled, conscious of the inadequacy of the new peach satin and lace robe she wore for Neil's benefit, and walked to Todd's bed. Turning down the covers, she held out her hand to him.

"I think you'll be more comfortable in bed," she said casually.

Todd ignored her hand but rose from the floor and reluctantly crawled up on the bed.

She studied him in silence for a moment, then sat beside him.

"No," she said as though no time had intervened since his hurtful words. "I'm not your mother. Your mother will always have a special place in your heart that I can never fill. I don't ever want to try to take that place away from her. But I love your father, and I want to love you. I want us to be a family. I want us to do things together, to be together, to love each other."

Todd lay back against the pillow and looked at her. "My mother died," he said, but she saw the glint of tears in his eyes. "She took too many pills and no-body came to help her and she died. And now I get to live with my dad all the time." He turned away from her and spoke in the same quiet voice. "Maybe you'll die, too."

She was cold, frigidly, piercingly cold in the flimsy lace and satin she wore. She reached out to touch the boy's shoulder, to comfort the pain she felt in his small body, but he tensed at her touch, shrugging away from her hand, locking himself away from her. She stood, backed a few steps from the bed, and then, because she could do no differently, she ran from his room.

And when she lost herself in Neil's arms, she didn't—couldn't—tell him what Todd had said. She clung to him fiercely, trying with all the power of her newfound love to hold on to the happiness they had known for such a short time.

Suddenly, the jangle of the telephone bell, its piti-ful wet-weather whimper, shattered through Ginnie's consciousness, bringing her a welcome reprieve from her memories. She snatched the receiver only to hear the all-too-familiar crackle of static. She waited for the noise to abate. She knew that it did no good to try to shout over it.

"Ginnie?" Cassie's voice fought with the static. "Can you hear me?"

"Yes," she called back. "Yes. Is something wrong?"

"That's my question," Cassie told her. "Listen, is that phone getting ready to go out again?"

"Probably," Ginnie answered lightly, but the reality of what it could mean to be without a telephone on this of all nights thickened her throat and muffled her voice.

"I thought they fixed it after the last rainstorm."

"So did I," Ginnie murmured. "Oh, so did I."

"What?" Cassie called. "Never mind. I'll talk quick just in case. Frank and I are getting ready to leave the parish hall, and it's snowing like a son of a gun. How would you like for us to come by and get you now? The roads might not be safe by tomorrow, and I hate to think of you having to spend Christmas alone."

Could she go with them? Could she spend the night on their comfortable sleeper sofa, practically under the Christmas tree, wake up in the morning to the delightful sounds of their three boys tearing into packages, just not be here if Todd came, not be here when Neil—

"No. No, thanks, Cassie." It wasn't hard to hide the tremor in her voice. The static helped. "But I'm almost ready for bed, and you know my Bronco will go anywhere. You and Frank had better get the boys home while you still can. I'll see you tomorrow afternoon."

"Are you sure? It's no trouble."

"I'm sure. Thank you, though."

"Ginnie?" She could barely hear Cassie's voice over the furious noises on the line. "Did you take care of that other problem?"

That other problem. "What? I can't hear you," she lied. Better this small lie than to risk explanation until she was certain what the explanation was, or to risk having Cassie and Frank disrupt their children's Christmas to ride to her rescue. "I'll talk to you tomorrow. Be careful going home."

That other problem, she thought as she sat at the kitchen table sipping now-tepid tea. She'd never told Cassie and Frank about Todd. They had moved to Pleasant Gap less than two years ago, after she had grieved for him, and long after she and Neil had divorced. They were a part of her new life, a life she had systematically and deliberately built for herself, a life into which she did not allow the past to intrude. They knew Neil's name, and Todd's name, and that she was divorced. And that was all that was necessary for them to know. It was who she was now that they had befriended. It was who she was now that they knew.

And it was a good life. After those hectic days in Little Rock, after the turmoil of her marriage, it was a good life. Her journalism students at the junior college liked her. Her youth group at the church did, too. Hardly a day passed without one of the kids popping in for a visit at this very table. She didn't have time to be lonely. And if it seemed as though she might have, there was always something to be done at the college, or the church, or a feature to write for one of the many state papers that occasionally carried her byline.

Time moved swiftly for Ginnie, and only at a moment like this could she pause long enough to wonder why it seemed so necessary that it do so. It was only at a moment like this that she could acknowledge what she had always known—that something was behind her, waiting for her to slow down so that it could catch her.

She spread her hands flat on the table before her and leaned her head on them. Slowly, as though in supplication, she stretched across the narrow table, gripping the opposite edge as a long, keening wail broke from her and she mourned what could have been.

Chapter 3

Damn you, Neil Kendrick. The accusation in Ginnie's words floated through Neil's thoughts as he made the necessary phone calls. He should have listened to his inner voice that told him something was wrong when he'd first got her message to call. He should have been more open to her instead of building his defenses, but, damn it, he never had been able to say what he felt to Ginnie. Why should this time have been different?

He'd heard the fear in her voice immediately and sensed, later, the tears she wouldn't now let him see. Would he be able to comfort her? Or would his presence, with both of them knowing that if he had listened to her earlier this might not have happened, tear them farther apart?

He found Kirk in the library, talking quietly with Carole Flannagan. Silently they walked with him to a secluded corner of the room. Carole had heard part of his conversation with the sanitarium. Kirk had not.

"Todd has run away," Neil said softly.

Kirk cast a startled glance at Carole but said nothing.

"He called Ginnie. He may be on his way there now. I'm going up to be with her until we hear something definite."

"How is she?" Kirk asked.

"She's frightened, but that's to be expected."

"How are you?"

Neil ran his hand through his hair and then clenched his fists at his sides, impatient with this show of weakness. "I'm fine. They were trying something new, taking him off all medication to see if they could get a clearer diagnosis."

Carole slipped her arms around him and hugged him to her.

"It will be all right, Carole. He's never gone far. He'll probably be back before I even get to Pleasant Gap. But if he isn't—"

"Things are under control here, Neil," Kirk interrupted. "Take all the time you need."

"And we don't have anything scheduled until after the first of the year," Carole added.

Take all the time you need. Todd will love you, too. Trust me. It won't be long. I'm sorry, Mr. Kendrick, I can't give you an answer now. Only time will tell how serious the damage is.

Had time run out? Neil didn't wait to change clothes. He grabbed a few things from his apartment, left Ginnie's telephone number with his answering service, and drove into the snow.

Ginnie and Neil. Ginnie and Neil. Ginnie and Neil. The branch against the window screen scraped out the words. The windshield wipers, fighting the ever-heavier snow, echoed them. They should have had the world in tow by now. Instead, it was crumbling around them, and there seemed to be no way to stop it.

Ginnie flung open the door to the bathroom, steamy from her quick tub, and stepped gratefully into the air-conditioned comfort of the bedroom. She was already wilting. The lights of Little Rock were just beginning to flicker on, and she paused at the window for a moment, looking over them, before she drew the drapes across the balcony doors. Dimly it registered that the season had again changed, and then with more clarity that it was June. June already. Almost a year had passed since she and Neil had first met, and where had it gone?

Hurried, she corrected. Hurried the way today had. Hurried, without time to stop and enjoy the quiet view. Hurried, without the luxury of peaceful time together. Hurried, with no way to cease the interruptions by the newspaper, Neil's law practice or Todd.

She heard the peal of the doorbell downstairs, and Charlie's one deep bark as she slipped into the coral silk dress she had bought for this evening. At least the sitter was on time. It wouldn't do for them to be late tonight.

"Aren't you ready yet?" Neil called from the door as she bent over her sandals, trying to buckle the straps.

She looked up at him sideways, through the mass of hair that had fallen over her face. God, he was beautiful—impatient, but beautiful—in his tux and tucked white shirt and gold studs. Just one kiss, Neil Kendrick, she thought, just a smile and one quick kiss and maybe she wouldn't feel like something he was dragging around because he had to.

His eyes darkened as he looked at her. "What's the matter?"

"Nothing." She fought the buckle into place and stood to look up at him. "It's just that I've never had dinner with a governor before."

And miraculously, the smile she had longed for softened his features. She waited expectantly while he crossed the room and took her face in his hands. "You're beautiful," he said, his mouth just inches from hers. "Have I told you that lately?"

She shook her head and waited silently for his kiss. It didn't come.

"I've been careless," he told her. "You'll shine like a jewel tonight." He grinned then. "But not if we're late." He snatched her shawl and purse from the bed. "Come on."

They were not late, and, with the pride he seemed to take in introducing her, she did feel as though she were shining. Her reporter's eyes made note of the subdued elegance of the governor's mansion, even knowing this could not be a working evening. It was not a large gathering, perhaps thirty people, and the men's faces were all familiar to her. She recognized several state legislators, a United States senator, a Supreme Court justice, an investor from Little Rock, an oilman from Texarkana, and, of course, the governor.

Neil selected a glass of white wine for her from a tray offered by a uniformed waiter. She concentrated on identifying and remembering which woman belonged with each influential man as she held the stemmed crystal in her hand and smiled, and made appropriate responses to gently probing questions, and laughed subtly at subtle jokes.

Dinner for thirty, with fine table linens, Waterford crystal, Lennox china, heavy sterling flatware and an undercurrent that at least the men seemed aware of. Ginnie would have been more comfortable with wine in plastic cups and pizza from a box in the back offices of the newsroom, but no one, except perhaps Neil, realized that as she flowed with the conversation around her. Only after the waiters had removed the dessert dishes and refilled the fragile cups did she allow herself to seek the comfort of Neil's thigh beneath the covering of the tablecloth. He captured her hand in his and squeezed it reassuringly. A common thread had become apparent to her. This was not a bipartisan gathering.

After dinner, they drifted into seemingly casual groupings, sipping drinks, while discreet music filled any silences. She and Neil were seated with a couple about their ages. The man was an attorney, like Neil, but he also served as state senator for a district in the Fort Smith area. The woman had been born to money and wore it well. The conversation was superficial, books and shows, nothing controversial, until a polite waiter delivered a message to Neil. With a slight apology, Neil and the senator excused themselves.

Discreet. That was the word for the entire evening, Ginnie thought. She looked around the room and stifled a laugh. And Victorian. Except for the waiters moving, discreetly, of course, through the room, she didn't see another man.

A silver-haired woman wearing ice blue and illusive, expensive perfume moved to sit beside her on the Chippendale sofa. Ginnie searched her memory for the woman's identity. Oh, yes. The investor's wife.

"Mrs. Kendrick, it's been delightful meeting you after all the complimentary things I've heard about you."

Ginnie smiled. She knew, somehow, that she must do that. And return the pleasantries. "Thank you, Mrs. Winston. I haven't yet had the opportunity to tell you how impressed I was by your fund-raising drive for the new wing at the Children's Hospital." What was she, Virginia Moore Kendrick, junior reporter for the *Arkansas Gazette,* doing, sitting on an antique sofa in the governor's mansion being complimented by the likes of Amanda Crowley Winston? And where was Neil?

"I must tell you what a refreshing and lovely addition you are to our political scene," Amanda Winston went on. "With you at his side, Neil should go far. This state senate seat will be only the first of many successes for him. Will you be resigning your position with the newspaper to help him with his campaign?"

Campaign? Senate seat? Ginnie kept her smile locked in place. *Resign?* If she had Neil alone right now, she would cheerfully wring his neck. "There have been so many decisions to make that we really haven't had time to weigh that one yet."

"Well, I admire your courage. Establishing a political career can be so taxing, even with a complete commitment by both partners. I know I would resent the time a campaign would take from my personal life."

What personal life? Ginnie thought, not letting a trace of bitterness show. The only time they had together they had to schedule, like this evening, or snatch furtively, late at night.

Another woman, brunette, a little older but not a great deal taller than Ginnie, wearing pastel green with an abundance of ruffles, joined the group. Ginnie searched her memory for that woman's identity—something—anything—to take her mind off the anger that she felt building. The wife of a congressman? Yes. From the northern part of the state? Heywood? That was it.

"That is a lovely dress, Mrs. Kendrick."

Ginnie directed her smile to the brunette. "Thank you, Mrs. Heywood."

"I have to know where you got it. It is so difficult to find petite clothes that don't make me look like an aging ingenue."

The senator's wife—Barre, was that the name? Ginnie was having difficulty remembering now—yes, Mrs. Barre—laughed delightedly. "Marybeth, ingenue maybe. Aging, never."

Gratefully, Ginnie felt the tone of the conversation shifting and the women relaxing around her. It was as though she had been initiated into an elite sorority, and, while she was a new member, a not quite known entity, she was to be accepted. Ginnie did not relax, though. She had been carefully taught her social graces by a strict but loving grandmother, and she now blessed the time she had once thought wasted on learning them.

She didn't allow herself to try to relax until after the men returned, until after polite good-nights had been said, until after she and Neil were alone in the privacy of their car, and even then she could not relax.

Neil remained silent while his mind raced over the avenues that had been opened up to him in that brief, intense and private conversation in the governor's library. He had suspected something, but not what had been offered—the endorsement of the retiring incumbent, the support of the party and financial backing, for this election, and for a much more important one in the near future. He had the talent and the charisma, they had told him. What he needed was some experience in the arena and a favorable statewide reputation.

In five years the senior United States senator would retire, and in five years Neil Kendrick would be groomed and ready for Washington. He smiled and let an old dream resurface, a dream he had been sure, until tonight, that the divorce and custody fight and Ann's needless death had destroyed. A lot of work faced him, but it would be worth it. Well worth it.

And Ginnie would love Washington—the challenge of getting there, and the challenge of staying there.

"Ginnie," he said softly.

"Mmm?"

"They want me—"

"To run for the state senate," she said emotionlessly.

He turned to look at her. She sat erect, feet together and flat on the floor, hands tightly clasped on the tiny purse in her lap, her shoulders squared, and tension obvious in every inch of her small frame.

"How—" He suddenly realized the obvious, that one of the women at the party must have said something. But why the tension?

"Thanks for keeping me in ignorance," she said in the same emotionless tone. "How much trouble would it have been to have given me a hint, just a little one, so that I wouldn't have had to sit there with a smile pasted on my face, pretending that I was in your confidence? Or was it that you didn't trust me not to run to my editor with the story?"

He bit back a quick retort at her show of anger, and at her lack of trust. "I don't know what you mean. I didn't know myself until tonight."

"Oh?" Sarcasm dripped from her, all the more scathing because it was so alien. "How strange. Everyone else seemed to know."

"For God's sake, Ginnie." She was almost impossible to talk to in one of her moods, and this one showed ominous signs of leading to a real standoff. "I knew something was up. I'm not stupid—"

"Thank you."

He ignored her thrust. "But the support, hell, the suggestion wasn't even made until we went into the governor's library tonight."

"Oh, yes. Just a cozy little dinner at the governor's mansion. Nothing elaborate. An every Friday occurrence, Neil?" She plucked at the skirt of the coral silk. "Just any old rag. We're among friends, people we have so much in common with."

Her voice rose. "Who was on display tonight? The candidate? Or the candidate's wife? Did I use the right fork? Did I laugh at the right jokes? Will I be an asset or a liability? And how did they vote? *Discreetly,* of course. Perhaps the way they would at an expensive auction? Close one eye for yes, both for no?"

"Stop it!"

He clenched the steering wheel. What idiot had presented it to her as an accomplished fact? He eased his grip and slumped back against the seat. There was probably a great deal of truth in the snippets of venom Ginnie tossed at him.

"Does it bother you?" he asked, needing her answer. "Being on display?"

"Yes! When I don't know what's going on and I'm expected to act as though I do."

She sighed and leaned against the seat, easing her temples with her fingers. "I can play games, Neil. Not well, and I don't like to, but I can. If I know the rules."

He felt the silence in the car as he pretended to concentrate on traffic. He'd never considered that she wouldn't be pleased by his news. He'd never considered that she wouldn't feel the same thrill at the challenge facing him.

He stole a glance at her. Huddled as she was, she looked tired. And defenseless.

"When did you decide you wanted to go into politics?" she asked.

She wasn't sniping at him now, but her hands still covered her face and he couldn't see her expression.

"A long time ago," he admitted finally. "Before law school."

"You never mentioned it to me."

He heard the hurt in her voice, in spite of her effort to hide it. It was something he'd heard too often in the past year not to recognize.

He expelled his breath and negotiated a left turn much too fast. "It didn't seem necessary to postmortem something that was never going to happen."

"Why, Neil?" He felt the soft caress of her hand on his shoulder. "Why wasn't it going to happen?"

He took one hand from the wheel and folded it over hers. Then he slid his arm around her and drew her to his side. She came, not melting, soft and loving as he wished, but she came, and he held her close while he tried to explain what he would have told her long before, had there been a reason for dredging up his disappointments.

"My major in college was political science," he told her. He felt her tensing and eased his hand along her arm.

"My father was the youngest judge ever elected to the Arkansas Supreme Court, and during my formative years, until he died, he made me aware of what the law should be, of what the law could be. And I managed to decide that my reason for being here was to make the world a better place. Through the law. It's not a unique idea. There are countless studious young men on campuses all over the world who feel the same way.

"But you can't do that with a bachelor's degree in political science, and you can't do it with a brand-new Juris Doctor in law, either. Even to be in a position to start to do something, you have to have experience, and contacts, and money, and a name. I had to work with the system, until I could get into the system.

"The Flannagans' tragedy was what convinced me that the time was right to make my first bid for election. They were clients of mine, a nice substantial middle-aged couple who went to church every Sunday, who, to my knowledge, never even got a parking ticket, who voted in each election and paid their taxes honestly, and who took great pride in their children.

They had two—a daughter, Carole, in college at Fay-etteville, and a son, Mickey, still in middle school.

"Carole came home early one Friday, while her parents were still at work, and found Mickey smok-ing a marijuana cigarette. She knew what it was."

He laughed bitterly, "Are there any kids today who haven't at least seen one? And he was already high enough so that when she asked him where he got it, he told her. A friend of his had a regular connection.

"He was thirteen, Ginnie, thirteen, and marijuana was readily available to him. Carole wanted him to put the cigarette down, put it out, flush it, but when she tried to take it from him, he went wild. She ran next door and called her father, who called an ambulance, who called the police. They all got there about the same time, but by then Mickey was unrestrainable. One of the policemen was little more than a rookie. He pulled his gun, and Mickey tried to take it away from him.

"In the struggle, the gun went off, and Mickey was killed."

They were nearing their house, but he turned down a side street, prolonging, if only for a few more min-utes, their time alone.

"When the authorities analyzed the marijuana re-maining in the cigarette, they found that it had been liberally laced with PCP, angel dust, and when Mickey's parents searched his room they found a bag, one that he had once kept marbles in, full of pills.

"And I had a cause. Get the drugs out of our schools. Keep our children safe. I decided to run for prosecuting attorney. It was the worst possible time I could have chosen."

Was now the time to talk about Ann? Ginnie had never asked, although he'd sensed at moments that she wanted to know more than the brief sketch of his marriage he'd given her.

"Why?" she asked.

He felt her yielding to him, her head against his shoulder, her hand sliding across his waist. Caught in the confinement of his arms, she was holding him.

"Ann," he said. He waited for her withdrawal, felt it beginning, and then felt her sigh back against him. He slid his hand to her hip and turned his head so that he could rub his jaw against the softness of her hair. He didn't want to bring Ann into Ginnie's life, but she was here already, and without this part the story made no sense.

"We were already having problems," he began, "had been since before Todd was born..." No. He wouldn't bring Ann into the car with them. Fool of Pulaski County, that's what he had been then. Ann had seen to that. Or perhaps he, with his zealousness, had made it so. Whatever the reason, it had taken a long time to rebuild his sense of self-worth, if, in fact, he had.

"Things came to a head early in the campaign." It wasn't enough, but it was all he could say. He wouldn't, *couldn't* dredge all of that up and throw it in front of Ginnie. Not now. Maybe not ever. "I withdrew from the race. A short time later, I divorced her."

Ginnie lifted her head from his shoulder, and he felt the comfort of her arms being taken from him. He tried to hold her to him, but she resisted, leaning away from him, looking at him.

"That's it?" she asked tightly. "You gave up a life-long dream because of a fight with your wife, and then you put the woman out of your life?"

"Not quite," he said, his voice as tight as hers.

"No, I suppose not." She turned to face the window. "Your dream is still with you. Is that story a warning for me, Neil? If I oppose the dream, will you send me away, too?"

"Ginnie—" Why couldn't she trust him, accept on faith that he loved her, without making him expose the anger, the sense of betrayal, the impotence he had felt?

"You're going to miss our turn," she said flatly.

He allowed himself the luxury of a stream of oaths as he negotiated the turn and slid to a stop beside the sitter's car. He turned to Ginnie, but she jerked the door open and was halfway across the lawn before he caught her. He touched her shoulder. She shrugged away from him, fumbling for her keys.

"All right," he said. "If that's the way you want it." He'd be damned before he'd beg her to understand.

The sitter was collapsed in the club chair in front of the television when Ginnie entered the living room, and looked as exhausted as Ginnie felt. She fixed her smile in place.

"A hard night, Mrs. Stemmons?" she asked pleasantly as the woman stood up.

"Not too bad, Mrs. Kendrick," she said, and laughed softly.

"Is Todd asleep?"

"I think so. He took two sandwiches and a bag of chips to his room about an hour ago, and I haven't heard anything from him since."

The dog raised his head, sniffing to identify the newcomers and then settled back comfortably in front of the couch.

"Did he take Charlie out?" Ginnie asked.

Mrs. Stemmons shook her head. "No, and I haven't had the heart to disturb the poor old fellow."

Ginnie heard Neil behind her. He would take care of paying the woman and seeing her to her car. "Thank you for coming this evening," she said, reaching for Charlie's collar.

She heard Neil speaking to the sitter as she led the dog from the room. Charlie could find the path on his own, but she needed some action to occupy her, and the dog responded gratefully to each small attention.

She led him to the back door, let him out into the fenced yard and stood quietly in the darkened kitchen. The light above the range illuminated only a small area, leaving the rest of the room in shadow. The light glowed on the coffeepot. She looked around hollowly. Her grandmother would have been proud of this kitchen. Somehow she had managed to measure a woman's success by her kitchen. This one was immaculate. It was efficient. It was tasteful. A Donna Reed kitchen, Ginnie thought bitterly. One that Harriet Nelson wouldn't be ashamed of. One in which Beaver Cleaver's mother could happily dispense coffee and platitudes. An old Mouseketeer rerun flitted across her memory, Annette and Jimmy singing "You Never Can Be Beautiful Beside a Dirty Sink."

Well, her sink wasn't dirty, but she didn't feel beautiful, not now. And she didn't feel successful, at least not in the one area that mattered. She choked back a sob. "Oh, Neil."

She reached into the cabinet for a cup, something, anything to do, and when she heard the kitchen door whisper open, she reached for a second one. She stood with her back to the room, every sense attuned to him as he came closer, every nerve throbbing as he stood behind her. She felt tears on her cheeks, and when he took her arms in his hands, she clutched the counter.

"What are we doing to ourselves?" she moaned in a broken voice.

"Ginnie." His voice caressed her as he turned her to him.

She let herself be drawn into the protection of his arms. If only she had the strength he had, if only she weren't so unsure of herself, then perhaps she could demand that they finish the talk only started in the car, but she didn't, and she wasn't. She slid her arms around him, under his jacket, loving the play of his muscles beneath her hands, the crush of his chest against her breasts as he kissed the tears from her cheeks.

And then it wasn't protection he was offering, or comfort. It was more, much more, as his lips moved across her face, tantalizing but avoiding her mouth, to her throat, to the swell of her breast barely visible in the starkly cut silk.

She heard the rasp of his breath and the thud of his heartbeat in the silence, matching hers, singing with hers, as he pressed her against the cabinet, following her, as at last he claimed her mouth with a possession that stole her breath from her and deprived her of what strength she had. She moved into his embrace, the hard ridges and planes of his body a wall against which she must cling, matching the deepening aggression of his kiss as she felt his hand sliding to her breast, cupping it. She melted against him, feeding on the love he offered. He was her life, her spirit, her reason for being.

The overhead light stunned her into awareness. Neil released her and stepped back so quickly she had to grab the counter for support.

"I'm hungry." Todd stood in the doorway, grinning.

Ginnie turned to the counter, trying to hide her flushed face and trembling hands from the boy. She poured coffee, almost, but not quite, managing not to spill it.

"You look super, Dad. How did it go tonight?"

She heard their voices behind her, soft, easy, conspiratorial, but the words wouldn't penetrate her numbed mind. No time. They never had any time, any privacy.

"I'm hungry, Ginnie." Those words penetrated. Two sandwiches, two, Mrs. Stemmons had said, and a bag of chips.

"There's the refrigerator, Todd." She spoke more sharply than she had intended, but couldn't stop herself, "I'm sure you can find something."

"Ginnie!" She heard Neil's indrawn breath before he spoke and knew that his shock was not at what she had said so much as the way she had said it. Why shouldn't he be shocked by her tone? She was.

"I'm—I'm sorry," she said, aborted passion, and anger, and frustration thickening her voice. "I'm . . . tired. Will you please let Charlie back in the house? I'm going to bed."

She couldn't look at Neil, but Todd's eyes caught hers as she stepped past him. They carried a smile, secretive and meant only for her. He knew what he had done, and he knew that she was aware of it. She ought to stay and defend herself, if with nothing but her presence, but she didn't want to have to defend herself. She wanted Neil to see past Todd's game playing, for him to defend her, for him to send Todd to his room, but instead he was angry with her. Well, she still had some pride. Neither of them would be able to read her defeat in the way she walked from the room.

She was in bed when Neil entered the bedroom, almost to the edge of her side of the king-size mattress. She had opened the draperies to the balcony doors and moonlight bathed the room. She wasn't asleep, she was too tense for that, but if she wanted to pretend, he wouldn't disturb her.

He undressed in the darkened room, glancing at her when his movements brought him near. She was so small and so—so damned *proud,* and right now, in her silent pride, she seemed younger and more defenseless than Todd. He wanted to go to her and hold her and see that nothing ever hurt her again.

He stubbed his toe in the dark and muttered an expletive.

And he wanted her to hold him, to show him with more than words that she did love him. That moment in the car had been precious for its rarity. Couldn't she see that he needed her to reach out to him? He sighed as he sank onto the bed, near the edge of his side of the mattress. Couldn't she see that he needed her support in the work facing him or the reasons for doing it dimmed to drudgery? Couldn't she see that this constant bickering between the two people he loved most was pulling him as no man should ever be pulled?

Her life, her spirit, her reason for being, Ginnie thought bitterly. Neil's tension communicated itself to her across the distance of the bed. And what was she to him? Had she ever known? In those first few weeks, she had been so entranced that she hadn't seen what was now becoming startlingly clear, that he put everything, *everything,* before her. Except when they made love.

She ached for his touch. If she turned to him now, if she slid across the bed to Neil, would he welcome her? The bed had never seemed so wide, but it wasn't nearly as wide as it would be if he rebuffed her and she had to return to this side.

"Neil," she asked hesitantly, "would it help if I quit the paper?"

He hadn't moved. Neither had she. Both lay on their backs staring at the ceiling. But she felt him growing closer.

"Do you want to?"

No, she didn't want to. Sometimes when she turned in what she knew was a particularly good story, she felt as if the newsroom was the only place where she had any true worth.

She couldn't say that, though.

"Mrs. Winston asked if I was going to resign."

She felt him shifting, turning toward her. "But do you want to?" he repeated softly. She swallowed and held herself still, fighting against turning toward him, fighting against begging him to take her in his arms.

"I don't want to stand in your way," she said. "If my resigning will help your campaign, I'll do it."

It was an overture, he realized, not the whole-hearted support he wanted, but he also recognized that for her it was a major concession. He willed her to come to him.

She grew uneasy in the silence, waiting for him to speak. She shifted, turning toward him. He lay propped on an elbow, watching her.

"You'd do that for me?" he asked. The words whispered and hung between them. "Why, Ginnie?"

Surely he knew. "Because I love you. Because above all else I want you to be happy."

She felt herself being drawn to him.

"Oh, Ginnie. Sweet Ginnie. You don't have to do that. Maybe later there will be so many demands on us it will be necessary, but not now. Not now. Now all I need is you beside me."

And then she was in his arms, crushed beneath him as she welcomed the fierce aggression of his mouth and the possession of his hands. They were everywhere, that marvelous mouth, those wondrous hands, bringing her life, bringing her love.

She felt the nightgown being drawn from her and, for one brief moment, the air-conditioning of the room, but that was no opponent for the heat Neil was building within her. She reached for him, touching him where she could, his back, his shoulders, his hips, feeling that her caresses were ineffectual but able to do nothing more. He moved lower. His hands were under her hips now, and his lips and tongue moved across her stomach, igniting fires, setting off small explosions deep within her. She caught his face with her hands and tugged him upward, needing his mouth on hers, moaning her need as he met it.

She moved beneath him. Too soon, it was too soon. She knew it. He sensed it and tried to draw back. She threw her arms around him, holding him to her, and arched against him. With a groan, he surged into her and then lay still, fighting for control.

"I love you, Neil," she said against his mouth as she began moving, urging him on. "I love you. I love you. I love you.

"Oh, yes," she moaned as he took control, murmuring words of love against her. Love me, her heart cried. Want me. Need me. "Oh, yes." He grew more demanding, his breath rasping in the darkness, his moans mingling with hers. He covered her mouth with his to silence their sounds. "Oh, yes." Make me believe it, she cried silently, even if it isn't true. Love me, Neil. "Ohhh, yesss."

Chapter 4

Ginnie stood at the kitchen sink tearing lettuce for salad. The kitchen was filled with the aroma of chicken stew, and the ingredients were measured, waiting to be combined for dumplings to be added to it. It was a miserable chill day in late October. All afternoon rain had threatened, and she knew that when it fell it would be cold and piercing, but she welcomed the touch of autumn. She hummed as she worked. Tonight, finally, Neil had a free evening at home.

The dining-room table was already set for three, with candles and an arrangement of daisies she had made time to pick up on her way home from the paper.

It seemed like weeks since they had had an evening together. Tonight should be—no, she corrected herself, tonight *would* be special. And later, after Todd had gone to bed, if the weather held—it was really too early, but perhaps they could build a fire in the fireplace and relax, together, in front of it with the wine she had chilling.

She looked over her shoulder as the swinging door whooshed open. Todd went immediately to the refrigerator, poured himself a glass of milk and slumped at the kitchen table, but he was smiling.

"Homework all finished?" she asked, smiling back.

He nodded. "Is that your chicken thing?" he asked. "Sure smells good."

The rain began pelting against the window, tight little drops that would sting and penetrate. A fire for sure, she thought. Cozy, warm and private, locking out the whole world, not just the rain.

"Can I go to the movies tonight?"

She frowned at the tomato in her hand and placed it carefully on the cutting board. "You know your father's going to be home tonight, Todd."

"Oh, well, yeah. But there's a super new movie at the Twin. A lot of the guys are going."

He sounded so wistful that she bit off her hasty denial. He'd been complaining for days that he never saw his father, but still, he was just fourteen, and for the most part a solitary fourteen. And it was Friday night.

"Who's going?" she asked.

"Oh, Tommy Wilcox, and Barry White, and maybe Joe Grimes. Can I, Ginnie?"

It wasn't her favorite group of kids. They were all at least a year older than Todd. Tommy already had his driver's license. But they were Todd's friends, she reminded herself again. Not hers. "What's playing?"

Todd mumbled his answer into the milk.

"What was that?" Ginnie asked, laughing.

"The Fiend From Black Forest Camp," he mumbled again.

She quirked an eyebrow at him. "I think we've had this conversation before, Todd." Twice, as a matter of fact, she remembered.

"Oh, come on, Ginnie. Everybody goes to those movies."

"Not quite everybody, Todd. I know one young man who is not going to go."

"Good grief! This one's supposed to be better than any of the *Halloween* or *Friday the Thirteenth* movies."

She kept her voice even. "And according to the movie critic at the newspaper, gorier than all of them put together, and with absolutely no plot."

He slammed his glass down on the table.

"Todd, I want you to go to the movies with your friends. I want you to have a good time. But I don't think films like that are healthy."

She returned to the cutting board, busying herself with the salad while she felt his glare boring into her back. She hated scenes like this. It would be so much easier just to say, Go ahead, Todd. Do what you want to. But somehow, someone had to establish the parameters for acceptable behavior, and somehow, someone had to start drawing this family together. And somehow, someone had to make those two goals one.

Suddenly the knife slipped and she pricked her finger—a little prick with a tiny drop of blood. She tossed the knife down and stood sucking on the wound. The sting was an insufficient excuse for the unhappiness roiling within her.

"When's supper?" Todd asked, and she noted with relief that the tension was gone from his voice.

"As soon as your dad gets home," she said. "Have you heard from him? I didn't think he'd be this late."

She sensed his presence beside her. "Is it a bad cut?" he asked.

"No. 1 am sorry about the movie, Todd. If it were some other film, if it were an evening when your father wasn't planning on being home, I'd say yes."

"Well . . . yeah. How about some homemade cookies?"

"Will that do it?" she asked.

"Not really," he said, "but I guess I can live with it."

"It's a deal. What kind?"

"Chocolate chip?"

"No chips. Peanut butter?" she countered.

Just then Ginnie heard a furious scratching at the back door, and she and Todd turned and spoke simultaneously. "Charlie."

She started toward the door, but he beat her to it, let the old dog into the house and knelt beside him, drying him with a towel he had grabbed from the counter.

"That's a good boy," he crooned as he worked on the dog. "We forgot all about you, didn't we, boy? It will be all right." He ruffled the animal's coat, warming him.

Ginnie leaned against the counter watching Todd's affectionate care of the dog. Seeing him relaxed and not defensive reminded her of the other times she had seen him this way and dulled the memory of his usually manipulative attitude toward her. He seldom asked her for anything, and homemade chocolate-chip cookies seemed such a small request.

"Do you want nuts in them, too?" she asked.

"What? Oh, the cookies. Why?"

"Because," she told him, "if I'm going to the store for chocolate chips, I might as well get nuts while I'm there."

His face broke into a big grin. "Of course I want nuts in them."

"Do you want to go out in the rain with me?" she asked. "Or do you want to stay here and make sure that supper doesn't burn?"

"I'll finish drying Charlie," he told her, "and I'll watch dinner for you."

At least the cookie-baking had been a success, Ginnie thought later that evening as she tidied the kitchen. She left the table set for three and the wine cooling in the refrigerator, but the chicken and dumplings had been held too long to salvage. She scraped the soggy mess into Charlie's bowl.

She heard the muted sounds of the television through Todd's closed door, but in spite of the late hour, she decided not to say anything about it. There was really no reason for him to have to get up early the following morning.

"Good night, Todd," she called to him.

Well after midnight, lying sleepless and alone in the expanse of the bed, she heard Neil's voice in the hallway and the soft murmur of Todd's response. A few minutes later, Neil entered the bedroom and closed the door behind him.

She watched his shadowy form moving quietly through the room as he struggled out of his shirt. She turned on the bedside lamp for him.

"You're awake," he said softly.

"Yes." The one-syllable word said nothing and yet said everything.

"I saw the cookies downstairs. It was nice of you to do that for Todd."

"I enjoyed it, and Todd seemed to. It wasn't quite what I had in mind for the evening, but it passed the time much better than just sitting around wondering what happened to you. I suppose something really important came up."

"You suppose?" he asked.

She sighed and swallowed, trying to ease the tightness in her throat, trying to keep the pain from her voice. "A phone call would have been nice."

"What are you talking about?"

"A phone call," she said dispiritedly. "Something simple like, 'Ginnie, I'm sorry, but I've run into something more important than keeping a promise to my wife and son. Don't wait supper. I'll see you sometime after midnight.'"

"You wanted a phone call, did you?"

She looked up at him sharply when she heard the anger in his voice.

"How many? And how badly did you want them? Obviously not badly enough to get home from work on time, nor to be here at the time when I said I would call back to talk to you."

"You called?"

"Twice, Ginnie."

"You called." Confusion muddled her thoughts. "But I was—here, except..."

"Except the two times that I interrupted meetings for the express purpose of getting in touch with you."

"But I—Todd didn't tell me."

"You should have asked him, Ginnie. It probably just slipped his mind. You know better than to jump to conclusions without checking your facts."

"Neil, I—" But she had asked Todd, and he had asked for the first time in months that she do something for him. No. She rejected the thought that crept into her mind. He didn't deliberately send her out of the house. He wouldn't have done that. Would he?

"Neil?" It was important that he understand. "I did ask him. Once about an hour after I got home from work, and again after I got back from the grocery store."

He stopped in his march to the closet and stood quite still. "Are you saying that my son lied to you?"

No. He wouldn't understand. There was no point in pursuing it much further. "I'm saying that one of the three of us lied—either him, or me. Or you."

He stood silently for a moment longer before whirling and going into the bathroom and slamming the door. She listened to the sound of the shower. When he came to bed, he said nothing else, and neither did she. That night, each lay alone, separated by more than the width of the bed, unwilling or unable to reach out to the other, but when Ginnie awoke the next morning she found herself a willing prisoner in his arms.

The even thud of his heartbeat and soft fanning of his breath against her forehead told her he still slept. Carefully, not wanting to awaken him, she pulled herself up on one elbow. His schedule of the last months had taken its toll. New lines crept out from his eyes. Even in sleep he seemed weary. As she watched, he frowned and stirred. Not awakening, he tightened his hold on her and pulled her closer, nestling his head against her breast.

A wave of compassion washed through her. Asleep like this he did not seem larger than life. He seemed defenseless, somehow vulnerable. In his sleep he held her as though he needed her. She could almost believe that he loved her as much as she loved him. Her eyes misted as she lowered her head to the pillow and held him cradled against her.

For this moment, at least, she could hold him. For this moment, at least, she was all he needed. For this moment, at least.

She held on to that moment for the days that followed, the weeks that followed, as one meeting after another took Neil away from home, as one emergency after another from his law practice ate up what time he didn't have scheduled for political conferences.

Todd, of course, went to see *The Fiend From Black Forest Camp,* after getting permission from his father without telling him that he'd been refused permission three times by Ginnie.

And he spent more time with Tommy Wilcox, Barry White and Joe Grimes, coming home from school later each afternoon after going directly to his father now with requests to study with his friends in the evening.

Ginnie knelt on the rug before the fireplace, alone in the house, again, except for Charlie who slept nearby.

Useless. That's what she was, she thought. And ineffectual—except at work and except for the big shaggy collie who responded so openly to affection.

She ran her hand over Charlie's coat, and he sighed with pleasure, but even that was an illusion. Charlie would welcome anyone's affection, but he only volunteered his own to Todd. She was an outsider even with the dog.

It wasn't a particularly important story. That was the irony of it. It was a sordid little tale of drugs and sex and violence that had erupted into murder. The trial was scheduled for Monday, the following day, in Fort Smith, and Ginnie had been given the assignment. The call from her editor had come only that afternoon, and in the emptiness of that dreary Sunday she had welcomed the assignment. But now, as she packed for the trip, she wondered at the wisdom of her going. She'd felt strangely free as she'd arranged with Mrs. Stemmons to come to the house for the several days she'd be gone. That feeling had persisted as she dragged down her suitcase and began going through her wardrobe. Was it normal to feel so liberated?

She tried to tell herself that she would miss her home, that she would miss Neil, but she knew that even staying here she would miss Neil.

She pushed down the lump in her throat and refused to think of that. Jury selection started early the next morning, and she had almost a three-hour drive facing her. She couldn't leave before Neil came home, yet for one fleeting moment she considered leaving him a note. It was petty, she knew, but she wanted him to feel the same sense of loneliness she did.

Neil stood in the doorway silently watching her as she bent over the suitcase unaware of his presence. A knot twisted in his gut as he watched her placing carefully folded clothes in the bag. He'd known she was unhappy, but, God, not this unhappy. He clenched his hands to keep from grabbing the suitcase and throwing it across the room. He couldn't let her leave. No matter what it took, he couldn't let her out of his life. She was his sanity, his lifeline, his stability.

"Where are you going, Ginnie?"

She had heard nothing before his softly spoken words, and caught in her own thoughts, she started guiltily. He was looking not at her, but at the suitcase, his face ashen, lines curving down to each side of his tightly held mouth.

"I—oh," she stammered in the face of his displeasure. "Fort Smith."

His gaze trailed from the suitcase to her face, and for a moment she saw mirrored in the warm satin brown of his eyes the same insecurity, the same pain she knew was in her own eyes, but only for a moment. His eyes narrowed and she was once again aware of his displeasure.

"Why, Ginnie?"

Anger rescued her. What right did he have to be so disapproving? She had barely seen him for months. She raised her head and squared her chin defiantly.

"Pete Wilkins broke his leg playing football yesterday. I'm going to cover the Higgins trial."

He turned from her so that she couldn't see the relief flooding through him. She wasn't leaving. He hadn't driven her away. And then his own anger, born from his fear when he thought he had, surfaced. What right had she to frighten him that way?

"Just like that, you're going? You did plan to say something before you left, didn't you?"

She sank onto the bed clutching a silk blouse to her, its texture the only softness in the room, in her life.

Her anger drained from her. She didn't want to fight with him—she never wanted to fight with him.

"Of course I planned to tell you, but I wasn't sure I'd have the opportunity. Unless I want to be driving all night, I have to leave soon, Neil, and I didn't know when you'd be home or where to reach you."

"I should have known you'd find some way to twist this around to make it my fault," he said. *Damn!* Why had he said that? That wasn't what he meant. What he wanted to do was take her in his arms and beg her never to frighten him that way again, never even to think of leaving him, but her head had jerked up belligerently at his words. She opened her mouth to speak, but he interrupted her.

"What if I said I don't want you to go?"

"*You* don't want me to go?" she asked incredulously. "Why not? You'll barely miss me, if you miss me at all. Will you miss me, Neil?"

He choked back an oath. If she knew just how much he would miss her, would she use that as a weapon against him? Or would knowing that he could be dependent upon anyone destroy the image that she had insisted on building of him? Either way, he couldn't run the risk.

"Is it the assignment, Ginnie? Or were you just looking for an excuse to run away from your responsibilities here?"

"Responsibilities?" she cried. "What responsibilities? Mrs. Stemmons will be preparing the meals and providing what custodial care Todd allows—that's all I do here, anyway."

Did she believe that? Could she really believe that? Neil jerked off his tie and threw it across the room. His words, carefully planned in the seconds his physical action required, refused to cooperate. All that came out was a hoarse, "You can't go."

She was on her feet instantly, in front of him, her face contorted. "Do you want me to quit my job, Neil? Is that it? If it is, say so, and we'll argue this right now. But if that isn't it, then I don't see any reason for what you just said. I have a job I love, a job that I held when I married you. I've offered to quit, but you told me it wasn't necessary. I have a master's degree in journalism, Neil. For God's sake, let me use it."

"I'm not stopping you from using your degree, Ginnie, or from using your brains. The Higgins trial could take a week. Or longer."

"I know." She was defeated again—by the closed look on his face, by her own warring emotions. She didn't want to be away from him a week, and yet something within her told her she needed this time away. If only he would say, Please don't leave me, Ginnie. I need you with me.

She hid her grimace as she turned, folded the blouse, placed it in the suitcase and snapped the latches closed.

"It's late, Neil. I have a long drive." If he would just take her in his arms and hold her, wish her safety for the trip, congratulate her on getting the assignment—*anything* except stand there silently, she wouldn't feel this misery.

She lifted the suitcase from the bed. He took it from her.

"I'll carry this down for you."

He carried the suitcase downstairs, then took it outside and placed it in the trunk of her car. She turned toward him hesitantly. It was all he could do not to carry her back into the house. It seemed that she stood there forever before she finally got in the car and drove away.

He watched until her taillights were no longer visible before he walked back into the house.

Todd looked up from a television program he was watching. "She's finally gone, is she?" He grinned. "Maybe she won't come back."

Todd's words were so close to his own thoughts that Neil could not tolerate them. He whirled on his son. "Don't you even think that, Todd."

Ginnie cried all the way to Fort Smith. Neil paced the house restlessly until just before dawn when he fell into a troubled sleep on the couch. Neither would have admitted their actions. If asked, neither could have explained them.

The week stretched endlessly for Ginnie. The trial was a tired cliché. It was difficult to believe from the boring way the case was presented that people's lives were at stake. Capital felony murder was the charge. The prosecution trudged through its steps, and the defense plodded along with no trace of the brilliance that Neil would have brought to a case with such ingredients. Ginnie found her motel room clean, impersonal and empty when she returned each evening. And no reporter in the courtroom needed a master's degree in journalism that week.

But there were moments. Ginnie and the other reporters gathered for lunch, sometimes for dinner, and shared tales of other assignments, or someone would recall a particularly good story another had written. Ginnie belonged with this group of people. Among them she felt accepted, welcomed and appreciated—

feelings she had almost forgotten. Feelings that didn't wane as the week and the trial drew to a close. They grew. And with them grew an awareness of the emptiness of the life awaiting her at home.

Home? She laughed bitterly. Her motel room, impersonal though it was, was as much home as their house in Little Rock had been for the last year.

And there also grew the awareness that no matter how much she loved Neil, she was losing herself in a morass of self-pity, frustration and neglect, and there seemed to be no way to save either her marriage or herself without destroying the other.

As she watched the trial's dispassionately told story of passions gone wild, her thoughts turned inward to her own passions, too long denied.

But I can't leave him. The thought so shocked her that she sat in stunned silence, missing an entire cross-examination. The witness was excused and another one called.

Or can I? He didn't need her, not really. If she stayed, she'd only destroy herself. She knew that.

But I love him. Was that enough? Had it ever been enough?

I need him. And she'd still need him, no matter what. But even remaining with him, she'd never have him. She might as well face that. He didn't need her. Todd didn't need her. Even Charlie didn't need her. Except in a perverse way that had nothing at all to do with *her* needs. She could stay in the house and become withered and bitter—she recognized the beginnings of that in herself already—or she could leave. And maybe away from him she could stop the pain she felt constantly.

If only there was some way to turn things around.
But she'd heard the subtle warning when he'd told her
about Ann.

She longed for her grandmother's ample bosom to
bury her face against and sob out her unhappiness, for
someone to be able to tell her what to do to make the
hurt go away. But there was no one, *no one,* who
could tell her what to do.

The people on each side of her stood, and she
looked up to see the judge leaving the room. The
prosecuting attorney was smiling. The defense attorney huddled with his client. And Ginnie had absolutely no idea what had just happened.

Friday arrived, bringing the inevitable conviction
and the end of Ginnie's week of respite. The reporters
got together for a late lunch and a drink before the
out-of-towners started for home, but Ginnie declined
their invitation to join them. She'd already packed her
car. It was time to face what awaited her.

When she reached the interstate highway, though,
she couldn't make herself turn onto it. She headed her
car south, instead, over once-familiar roads.

The mountains spread out before her, gentle blue
shadows rising around the rim of the valley. Her destination was a tiny town just over the first ridge. Once,
she'd thought those mountains shut her away from the
rest of the world. Now she saw them differently. They
were a protective barrier holding back the harshness
of the world.

She crested the first ridge. The road hesitated
downward before gathering itself for its climb up the
second, and she turned off the highway onto a nar-

rower asphalt strip. A mile later she was in the center of what was left of the small town.

A pair of two-story rock buildings, boarded over now, remained to guard the shell of a third that had long ago succumbed to neglect and vandalism. A prefabricated metal building housed the town's only business, a combination grocery store, gas station and bait shop for the nearby lake. There was a small redbrick post office, and a still smaller yellow brick building housing telephone-company equipment. A gaunt hound wandered unconcernedly across the street in front of her car. She had a picture in her scrapbook of the town as it had been fifty years before when the coal mines were still going strong and the rock buildings had held a bank, a hotel and a thriving general store. Otherwise, she would not have believed the prosperity that this town had once known.

Ginnie turned off the main street. Two blocks away on a small ridge, the house still kept vigil over the dying town. She slipped the car into Park and sat looking up at the building. Memories of the smells of homemade bread, cookies hot from the oven and her grandmother's beef stew carried her back to the time when she had spent hours in a swing hung from a now-missing limb of the giant oak in the front yard and planned what she would do with the wonderful future awaiting her. A rusted car body now occupied the swing's place in the midst of an overgrown lawn. What shutters remained on the upstairs windows hung precariously.

Allowing the house to be sold in the probate of her grandmother's estate six years before had seemed her only alternative at the time. The money had helped finance her college education. Besides, with her grandmother gone, she'd thought there would be no reason for her ever to want to return to the house.

She brushed absently at the tear sliding down her cheek and eased the car into gear. There were no answers here.

Two miles farther into the hills, on the way to a larger but no more prosperous town, lay a well-tended cemetery. Ginnie avoided the familiar white-frame church, taking the narrow road which bordered the outer perimeter of the graveyard until she reached a large pine tree. She parked, stepped from the car and walked among silent, ancient markers until she reached a plot outlined by a wrought-iron fence.

She leaned against the fence, not opening the gate, and not going inside. A wild rose grew in one corner of the plot, twisted and leafless now in winter's chill.

"When you're in trouble you go to family, don't you?" she asked of no one. Well, here was her family—a grandfather she had never known, a mother and father who she remembered only as shadowy dream figures from her distant childhood, an aunt and an uncle who had both died in infancy and a grandmother who had been father, mother and friend to her for too few years.

"Tell me," she whispered. "Tell me how to make the hurt stop. Kiss it and make it go away, Gran."

Her grandmother had known enough hurt of her own. She'd buried her husband and her three children. But she'd found a calmness Ginnie had never understood, drawing strength from Mass each Sunday and nurturing a small child, in loving and caring and giving, teaching the child values she had learned fifty years before. *You have to be true to yourself, Virginia*. That was the important one, Ginnie knew.

But the others—*Home and family are all-important.
The most important thing you can do in this life is to
be part of a family. To love and to care for someone
else is all there is once you strip everything down to its
basics.*

"Tell me how, Gran," Ginnie whispered. "I can't
do it alone."

There was no answer, only a shifting of the wind. A
snowflake fell on her face, and then another, and another. She looked around the bleak cemetery and then
back at the neat stones commemorating her family.
They had a closeness—had it even in death—that she
and Neil, and Todd, would never know.

After a few brief spits, the snow stopped, melted
before it even touched the ground.

No answers. There were no answers anywhere.

Ginnie got back in her car and reluctantly turned it
toward Little Rock.

Chapter 5

Neil's car was not at home when Ginnie arrived. Of course not, she thought bitterly. How foolish of her to have hoped it might be. A strange car, one long over-due for a paint job and nosing downward because of oversize rear tires, sat blocking access to her side of the garage. She parked beside it and lifted her suitcase from the back seat.

The television's blare was her only greeting when she let herself in the front door. She made no attempt to be quiet, but she doubted that she could have been heard over the din even if she had yelled.

She set her suitcase in the entry hall, stepped around the couch and pushed the button on the television, silencing its clamor. She glanced at the clutter on the coffee table, at the four plates obviously just used and left dirty and discarded in the living room. She heard laughter from the kitchen, as abruptly silenced as the television sound. She reached the kitchen door just as it opened. Todd and his three now-inseparable companions marched out. Joe looked uneasy, Todd, Barry and Tommy merely defiant.

"What are you doing here?" Todd asked.

She smiled humorlessly. She'd not expected a warm welcome, and she certainly hadn't gotten one. "I live here. Remember? What's going on?"

"Nothing," Todd said. "I'm spending the night at Tommy's."

Before she could speak, he added, "Dad said I could."

She raised an eyebrow but said nothing. He pushed past her and led his friends through the house, slamming the front door on his way out.

She expelled her breath upward and shook her head, trying to free the hair from across her forehead and the unwanted thoughts from her mind.

"Welcome home, Ginnie," she said to the empty house. "It's so nice to see you again. The week seemed endless without you."

Her breath caught in a sob, but when she pushed open the kitchen door, it ended in an expletive as she surveyed her normally spotless kitchen. What would have happened if Mrs. Stemmons hadn't come in each evening? she wondered as she realized that the mess facing her was all new.

Potato chips spilled out across the cabinet from a ripped-open sack. A drying mess still recognizable as stew splattered the stove top and counter, while on the stove a pan held the scorched remains of what had probably been intended for dinner.

Ginnie stood in defeat in the midst of dirty glasses and silverware, wadded paper towels, open cans of vegetables and spilled, half-empty pop bottles.

"See, Ginnie," she said finally in a small, tight voice. "You are needed, after all."

She grabbed a handful of the wadded paper towels to throw in the trash and as she did she noticed the bottle of wine she had bought weeks before for the celebration dinner that never took place. It was empty now, except for the cork, which looked as though it had been pushed down into the bottle. She retrieved it from the trash and set it on the counter. Had Neil done that? she wondered. It didn't seem likely. He appreciated good wine too much to have ravaged the cork in that manner.

But suddenly it didn't matter. What mattered was the knowledge that she didn't belong, had never belonged, and no matter what she did, would never belong. If all they needed was a housekeeper, they could hire one. A housekeeper didn't have to feel responsible for anything other than tending to the mess a family made of their house. A housekeeper didn't have to feel the pain of knowing that's all she was.

She couldn't stay in this house any longer. Even the air in it seemed bent on pushing her out. She felt tightening pressure in her chest, her throat and behind her eyes, but she swore she wouldn't cry, not now. She fumbled in her shoulder bag for her notebook. Her hand jerked as she scrawled the note. *Neil, I can't take it anymore. I'll let you know later where I'll be.*

She shoved the mess on the counter to one side with a crumpled dish towel and lay the note there in isolated splendor. Then she plopped the empty wine bottle onto one corner of it to hold it secure.

There was no need even to go upstairs. On her way back through the living room, she picked up her suitcase and carried it with her from the house.

She drove for hours, aimlessly, unable to decide where to go. Several times she almost took the interstate west, back to Fort Smith, maybe even back to the town where she had grown up, but she couldn't bring herself to do that. There was nothing for her there. She drove through areas of Little Rock that she had never seen before, and she didn't see them this time, either.

Her mind played over all the scenes that had hurt her in the past year, but it wouldn't stop with that. Then it replayed the good times. It replayed the moment she had held Neil while he slept and he had seemed vulnerable. It replayed the feel of his skin against hers, the taste of his mouth, the hard pressure of his body.

And during that endless evening, she did cry, silent tears that streamed down her face. She beat the steering wheel in her frustration. She raged aloud at the futility of it all.

After her tears dried, after some of the swelling around her eyes had subsided, she looked around trying to find out where she was. She'd gotten only as far as Jacksonville—so few miles. She pulled into the Holiday Inn parking lot, meaning to take a room, but went into the restaurant instead.

She'd had no lunch, and no dinner, but she didn't think she could face food. She offered an attempt at a smile in response to the waitress's cheerful greeting and ordered coffee.

Two cups, three, four later, she sat alone, the only customer at that late hour, and knew that while she no longer had a marriage, she couldn't leave Neil with no more than a note.

Ginnie parked in the driveway next to Neil's car, hesitating before she let herself into the darkened house.

The remains of a fire glowed from the hearth, but other than that, the house was dark as well as quiet. She stared into the glowing embers. How anticlimactic everything was, she thought. She'd just made the hardest decision of her entire life, and the person she needed to tell that decision was probably already asleep.

She muffled a twisted laugh. How did she handle this? Did she make herself a bed on the couch? Did she turn around and leave again? Or did she go upstairs and say, Excuse me, I'm going to share your bed tonight but I'm going to leave you?

"Where in the hell have you been?"

Neil's words cut through her rising hysteria. She whirled to the sound of his voice. Accustomed now to the darkness of the room, she saw him in the shadows of the wing-back chair. She watched the darker shadow of his arm reach upward to the lamp on the table beside him, and light pooled over that corner of the room.

He looked awful, she thought as she finally saw him clearly. He'd shed his coat and vest and tie. His collar was open, his shirtsleeves rolled up, and his hair had lost its styled perfection and hung errantly over his forehead. A day's growth of beard darkened his jaw. He held an almost empty glass negligently in his left hand. The scotch bottle waited on the table.

"I asked you a question," he said, and she sensed the slight slurring of his words more than she heard it.

"Are you drunk?"

He looked at the glass as though he had forgotten it and lifted it to his mouth. "No such luck, dear wife," he said before draining the glass. "But I'm working on it."

He slammed the glass on the table. "Where have you been?"

She had thought her decision hard to make, but the effort of making it had been nothing compared with the agony of now telling him of it. "Driving."

"Just driving?" he asked. "Was that safe?"

"I don't understand."

"Good," he said, unwinding from the chair. "That makes two of us. My wife has been gone for a week. On the evening I expect her home, I come back to a disaster area and find this—" he snatched her note from the table "—under an empty wine bottle. What was it, Ginnie? A fit of self-pity? God knows, Todd left it a mess here. Did you sit there drinking the wine thinking how hard your life was, how empty your life was, how meaningless you life was? How long did you take to make that decision, Ginnie. One glass? A half bottle? All of it?"

He splashed more scotch into his glass. "Well, here's to some liquid courage."

He set the glass down without drinking from it. "Only mine doesn't seem to be working, and yours has apparently worn off."

He walked to the fireplace and stood facing the mantel. "Oh, hell, Ginnie." He gripped the ledge for long seconds before turning to face her. When he spoke, his voice reflected none of that brief burst of emotion. "Why did you come back?"

At that moment she loved him more than she ever had, and she hated him for making what she had to say a necessity.

"I thought you deserved more than a note." There was no easy way to say it. "I want a divorce, Neil. I won't do anything until after the election, but we don't have a marriage, and I can't go on pretending that we do."

"A divorce. You've been around the law long enough to know that if that's what you really want, there's nothing I can do to stop you. But I can't accept that we have nothing left."

"I'm sorry."

"Ginnie, you need a clear head to make a decision like that."

Did he really think she had been drunk? "I didn't drink the wine, Neil. I found the bottle in the trash. And I didn't make this decision lightly."

She felt tears starting again and was powerless to stop them.

"We don't have a marriage," she repeated. "We don't have a family. And no matter how much I love you, I can't ignore that any longer. If I didn't love you, I might be able to stay."

His voice was incredibly gentle. "You know you aren't making any sense. You're leaving me because you love me?"

She looked up at him leaning against the fireplace wall. Maybe it didn't make any sense, she thought. She tried to read in his face one sign to help change her mind. Not arrogant now, he seemed puzzled and hesitant. Her gaze traced the line of his shadowed jaw and rested on the cleft in his chin. Imperceptibly, almost, and so fast that had she not been watching at that instant she would not have seen it, a quiver moved across his face.

"Oh, Neil," she moaned. "If I didn't love you, it wouldn't hurt so much."

He pushed away from the wall and started toward her. She couldn't move as he circled the couch and took her coat from her, draping it over the back of the sofa.

"What wouldn't hurt so much?" he asked, taking her shoulders in his hands as she stared at him, unable now even to speak.

He traced one finger along her cheek. Infinitely gentle, he bent toward her. "Does this hurt, Ginnie?" His lips touched hers. "Or this?" he whispered, sliding an arm behind her and pulling her closer. "Or this?"

She moaned against his mouth, powerless under the assault of her feelings as he drew her to him, as his mouth claimed hers, as his hands moved over her with a sureness born of knowledge of her body. Soon she would be lost in him. Even now she fought to keep her hands from creeping around him. Even now she fought to keep from deepening the kiss. Even now she found herself forgetting her pain in the pleasure he could bring her, in the mindless ecstasy of loving him.

"No!" She pushed away from him. "Can't you see? This won't solve anything."

He dropped his arms to his sides. "I've missed you, Ginnie. This whole long, miserable week, I've missed you."

There! Wasn't that what she'd wanted to hear? And yet now it seemed so inadequate. "And I've missed you, Neil. These whole, long, miserable months."

She ran her hand through her hair, fighting her heart's demand that she throw herself against his strength. "Please don't make this any harder than it already is."

"Christ!" he swore. "What am I supposed to do? Just let you walk in and make your announcement and leave? Without saying anything? Without trying to stop you?"

She had to do something, something physical. She couldn't stand rooted to that spot any longer.

"I'm going to make some coffee," she said. "I think we both can use some."

His face hardened as he stepped away from her. She couldn't bear to look at him any longer. She headed for the kitchen but came to an abrupt stop just inside the door. Order had been restored—it was far from perfection, but Neil had made an effort. Her throat tightened.

"Too late," she moaned. "Too late."

He came into the kitchen as she finished filling the coffeepot and stood silently watching her. Her hand shook. She couldn't remember how much coffee she had measured into the basket.

"Have you eaten?" she asked.

"What—no."

"Are you hungry? Do you want something to eat?"

"What I want is for you to quit messing with that damned coffeepot and tell me what happened in your head today."

She leaned her cheek against the cabinet door. "It isn't just today, Neil. And it isn't just in my head."

She felt his hands on her shoulders, strong hands, kneading at her tension.

"Please don't," she whimpered.

"Don't touch you?" he asked. "Don't care for you? Don't ask? Don't what, Ginnie?"

"Don't do this now. You've shut me out for so long, don't do this to me now."

His hands stilled. "I never meant to shut you out."

"But you have. And maybe you won't mean to, but you will again. There will always be another client, another meeting, another election—that's what matters to you. You don't need me, Neil, except . . ."

She had been going to say, except in bed, but she couldn't. That wasn't true, either. Wouldn't another woman, someone who could accept this life, perhaps even appreciate it, be better, in bed as well as out of it, for him?

"You don't need me, Neil," she repeated. "Todd doesn't need me. Charlie doesn't need me. No one needs me."

"You're what holds it all together. Don't you see that?"

"No! I don't see anything at all like that. What I see is that everything else in your life takes precedence over me. And I need more than that. I need a husband, Neil, not someone I see occasionally, late at night. I need a family, not a child who resents me. I need a home, one that I feel is my home, not one in which I'm merely tolerated."

He twisted her around to him. "You have that, Ginnie."

"No." She shook her head, her eyes never leaving his. "I have nothing, except an emptiness that I can't make go away, an emptiness that only worsens when I catch a glimpse of what our life could be.''

"And if I could give you what you need?''

"Don't. Oh, God, don't say that. Please don't say that. Because you can't. Everything is against it.''

"And if I could give you what you need?'' he repeated.

Could he? Could he do that? If only he could. Ginnie swayed against him, not in surrender but in the weakness of her need to believe him. He enveloped her, his arms circling her slender body, his presence pervading her soul.

"Please.'' With a whimpered plea, she turned her face to his. Even she didn't know what she meant. Please don't hurt me anymore. Please love me. Please make me believe. "Oh, please.''

He feathered kisses across her eyelids, her forehead, her temples. "Trust me, Ginnie,'' he groaned as his mouth claimed hers.

The kiss held all her desperation, her longing, her need. When he lifted her to hold her against him, she knew her surrender was complete. She couldn't leave him. Not now. Maybe not ever. Through the riot of sensations flooding through her, she felt silent tears creeping from beneath her tightly closed eyelids. "Oh, please.''

The shrill chirping of the alarm beckoned Ginnie back to consciousness the next morning. She fought it, as she always fought it, mumbling incoherent protests as Neil disentangled himself from her and turned to the clock, but he only silenced it, moved back to her side and wrapped his arms around her. She murmured a wordless sound of pleasure and snuggled into his warmth.

When she awoke again, she was alone in the wide bed. She ran her hand over the sheet beside her. Not cold yet, it still bore the lingering traces of Neil's warmth. Reluctantly she opened her eyes and looked around the empty room. She caught a glimpse of movement out of the corner of her eye and turned toward it. Her welcoming smile froze as she realized that Neil was dressed in dark slacks and a cream-colored cable-knit sweater. His dark hair was neatly and correctly in place, and she scented the aroma of freshly applied after-shave lotion.

He smiled hesitantly and walked to the bed, dropping onto it to sit beside her. He traced a slender finger along her bare arm and then covered her with the sheet, tucking it around her.

"You don't have to get up now," he said.

"Where are you going?" At least, she thought, he had the grace to look uncomfortable.

He sighed. "I have to go into the office this morning."

She turned from him and lay flat on her back, studying the ceiling. "I see," she said emotionlessly.

"No, Ginnie, you don't see." He turned her toward him. "I have a trial starting Monday. I have some things I have to do today, but I'll be back as soon as I can. I promise you that."

She looked into the depths of his eyes, trying to read in them the answer to a question she had to ask herself if she never spoke the words aloud. Had he meant what he said the night before? If he hadn't, why had he bothered to lie? She felt a wrenching in the area of her heart. And why was it so desperately necessary for her to believe him?

"I promise," he said softly. "We'll have most of the afternoon, and tonight, I'll talk to Todd."

She reached out to him, tracing her fingers along his jaw. He caught her hand and placed a soft kiss in her palm.

"Trust me, Ginnie. I'll find a way."

The next week seemed a return to the familiar routine, but with undercurrents of intense differences. Outwardly, their schedules seemed unchanged. Ginnie went to work each morning, Neil to the office, and Todd to school. There were still evening meetings, but Neil cut them short, even managing on one occasion to be home for dinner, and on two others to be home before Todd went to bed. And Todd—Todd seemed different, almost subdued. Ginnie wondered about the talk Neil had had with him. Neil, too, was subdued. No, not subdued, she thought. Preoccupied. And she couldn't help wondering if he resented the time he was spending at home with her. Several times she became aware of him watching her, but she realized that those occasions were no more often than the times she spent watching him, lost in thought, his heavy eyebrows drawn together with deep lines marring his forehead.

By unspoken agreement, neither mentioned what had happened, or what had almost happened, the previous Friday. But Ginnie felt the tension growing as the week drew to a close, as another Friday came, and went, as another Saturday morning approached.

Trust me, he had said, yet she saw no real change, no real reason for her trust except as an exercise in blind futility.

* * *

Ginnie moaned in protest as the alarm chirped its summons. She felt the subtle shift of the bed as Neil turned to silence the clock and then his arms around her as he dragged her into his embrace.

"Wake up, sleepyhead," he whispered in her ear. He teased little kisses across her face before catching the corner of her upper lip between his, tugging gently and flicking a teasing caress across her lip.

She opened one eye and peered at him. "Don't you have to go to the office?" she asked suspiciously.

He shook his head and shifted his weight so that he poised balanced above her, propped on an elbow on each side of her, smiling down at her. "No."

"Or a meeting with the election committee?"

"No."

She couldn't believe it. There hadn't been a Saturday in months when he hadn't had to run off somewhere. She smiled up at him lazily. "Then why did you set the alarm?"

He raised himself, freeing one hand to trace lightly down her cheek, her throat, her breast—lower still, along the indentation of her waist, to her thigh, creating quivers of anticipation each place his fingers lingered.

"It might seem unromantic to set the alarm, but with our schedules the way they are, I wanted to make sure we had plenty of time for this," he said lightly. "Do you know how long it's been since we've spent a morning together?"

She nodded silently, acutely aware that his hand had stopped its trailing. His mouth hovered a heartbeat away from hers.

"Kiss me, Ginnie," he whispered.

It was all the invitation she needed. She slid her arms around him and raised herself to meet his embrace.

As absorbed in Neil as she was, she barely heard the click of the door, but the blare of televised cartoons as the door thrust open silenced the clamor within her. She shrank away from Neil as he muttered an oath and, grabbing the sheet, covered himself and rolled over to face the door. Ginnie didn't look. She knew Todd stood there. What she didn't know was how much he had seen in that brief moment. She barely recognized Neil's voice as he spoke with controlled anger.

"Didn't you ever hear of knocking and waiting to be told it was all right to enter a room?"

"Gee, Dad. I'm—I'm sorry."

But Ginnie heard no sorrow in those words. She hoped it was her imagination, but what she heard was a sneaky little pleasure in having interrupted what had to be, for Todd, an illicit scene. And then she hated herself for attributing those kinds of motives to a fourteen-year-old boy.

The door closed, silencing the televised sounds. Neil groaned and rolled onto his back, reaching for her hand.

"Ginnie, I'm sorry."

She withdrew her fingers from his, sat up and fumbled for her robe at the foot of the bed.

"I guess I should say it's all right," she said as she cinched the belt around her waist.

"No, it isn't all right."

"No, it isn't, is it?" she said and walked with rigid control into the bathroom.

When she emerged later, bathed, carefully made-up and dressed protectively in slacks and a sweater, she found Neil dressed similarly, seated on the unmade bed speaking on the telephone. He looked up at her but did not smile as he replaced the receiver. Instead, he stood, went to the closet and pulled a suitcase from the top shelf.

"Mrs. Stemmons is coming over for the weekend," he said as he began rummaging through the closet. "And we're doing something we should have done long ago. If you want to," he added as she continued to stand there silently.

She smiled, hesitantly at first, and then in genuine pleasure. "Just the two of us?"

He nodded wordlessly.

She didn't even ask where they were going. She didn't care, so long as the two of them could be alone together.

They drove north, following the interstate until it veered westward, only then stopping for breakfast. Ginnie felt strangely shy as she sat across the booth from Neil, and a little guilty for feeling so free from mundane responsibilities. Two days, she thought. Two whole days with no one but Neil.

When they returned to the car, she scooted across the seat to his side without waiting for his invitation. He draped his arm over her shoulder and hugged her close. This was how it should be, she thought as she sighed contentedly against him, and he headed the car north, into the mountains.

The road climbed steadily, past pines encroaching on the edge of the well-kept highway shoulders, slicing through rock ledges, with occasional gaps in the trees affording a view of the mountains surrounding them and in the distance. They weren't the Rockies, of course. Nothing so spectacular. The Ozarks were neither high enough, nor harsh enough, ever to be mistaken for the Rockies, but they had a rugged splendor of their own—blue and violet-hazed in the distance, green and untamed on either side of the road, reminiscent of her childhood yet much more imposing than the hills where she had grown up.

The river valley was far behind them, until they crested a hill and were in another river valley, a high one. A green and white highway sign announced their location: Pleasant Gap, Arkansas. Population 2,107.

Another green and white sign, this one with an arrow, marked the route to the business district. Neil grinned at her as he slowed the car then turned off the highway onto the narrow road leading to the town. But even this road did not lead through the center of town. A still narrower street did that, cutting through rows of neat, small, freshly painted buildings in a hodgepodge of architecture, all old, to a tiny square.

Neil pulled the car into a parking place, the only empty one Ginnie could see, and turned off the ignition. Ginnie glanced at him, puzzled but delighted, as he pocketed the keys.

"Do you want to go for a walk?" he asked. "I don't think it will take long to see it all."

She smiled and nodded, eager to explore this miniature town. A red stone courthouse dominated the middle of the square. It was by far the largest building in town, but even it was no larger than—no more than—*a dream,* Ginnie thought. The courthouse lawn, at the widest only six feet, neatly trimmed, led out to a narrow sidewalk banding it. A slender monument,

the inevitable commemoration to the Confederate
army, stood at an angle in one corner. On the opposite corner, one tree, bare now, stood guard over one
wooden bench. Streets that would never accommo-
date the width of two cars led one-way traffic around
the square. One each side, brick buildings in various
colors, all narrow, all tall, faced equally narrow sidewalks. Even the crosswalks were miniature, she noted,
barely wide enough for the two of them to walk side
by side.

The stores bustled with activity. Saturday-morning
shoppers crowded the square, and traffic moved un-
ceasingly around it. Somehow she was surprised to see
that the people on the sidewalks with them were
normal-size people.

"I keep looking for the Yellow Brick Road," she
said, grinning.

Neil glanced down at her, puzzled, before the
meaning of her words brought a laugh from his throat.

"This has to be Munchkinland from the Land of
Oz," she said. "I only hope that if we meet up with a
witch, it's the Good Witch of the East."

Neil kept her arm tightly tucked within the con-
fines of his own and, as leisurely as they could with the
crush of people about them, they window-shopped
their way around the square, to a drugstore on the
opposite side of the courthouse from where they had
parked the car. Through the window, Ginnie saw a
long counter and booths lining one wall. She glanced
a question at Neil, and he led her inside the store, to
an empty booth, seated her and returned a few moments later with two cups of coffee.

Ginnie noticed glances in their direction, people
obviously trying to place them, and realized quite

happily that no one could. The chance of running into one of Neil's clients or political associates were almost nonexistent.

"I love this place," she said as he sat down beside her. "How on earth did you find it?"

He took a long drink from his coffee. "I think it found me, Ginnie, while I was looking for something else." He toyed with his cup before speaking. "Do you think you could be happy here?"

She paused with her cup midway to her lips. "Why?" she asked breathlessly.

He reached across the table, took the cup from her hands and then took her hands in his. "Harve Perkins, the circuit judge for this district, had a heart attack last month. He's retiring because of it. Someone will have to be appointed to fill out his unexpired term. I've already been told that I can have the job if I want it."

"But—but—the election?"

Neil shook his head. "I've withdrawn from the race."

"Neil—" Ginnie noticed the curious stares of those around them and lowered her voice. "Neil, this election was the chance of a lifetime for you. You can't give up something like that."

"I already have," he said. "What I can't give up is my marriage, you and my son. I never had a home when I was growing up, Ginnie. My mother died giving birth to me, and my father never remarried. He made the law his whole life, what life he really had. I don't want that for myself, and I don't want that for us. Right now you're more important to me than anything I *might* be able to do for the state of Arkansas or anything I *might* be able to do for the country."

"And your law practice? Do you have to give that up, too?"

"Let's get out of here," he said. "We need to talk."

They found a park on the outskirts of town, deserted except for one squirrel who scurried down a tree and chided them raucously for not having brought him any food.

Ginnie sank onto a wooden bench and waited until Neil settled beside her.

"You've worked hard to build your reputation, Neil. Can you really give it up? Give up the excitement and the adulation, and the . . . the money?"

He leaned against the slatted back of the bench, hands thrust in his pockets and legs stretched out. "I don't know. I've tried to be as honest about it as I can."

He laughed. "Kirk thinks I'm crazy. Maybe I am, a little. But if we stay in Little Rock, there's going to be something constantly intruding on our private lives—friends or business, or just the pace of living there.

"A circuit judgship isn't the end of the world, Ginnie. And neither is Pleasant Gap, Arkansas. Maybe I won't be trying the cases, but I'll be hearing them, I'll be ruling on them. I'll be involved with them.

"And here, maybe, we can have the kind of home that you need, and that I need, and that Todd needs. And eventually, not much longer now," he promised, "the children you want, *our* children.

"The change won't be easy, but I'm willing to try."

He turned to her, taking her face in his hands. "I have to try it, Ginnie."

"Oh, Neil." She leaned against him, sliding her arms around him. "Of course we have to try. And it will be wonderful," she promised. "It will be wonderful."

Chapter 6

And it was wonderful, for a while. The house they found a few miles out of town, a low, rambling one-story bungalow, seemed perfect in spite of its disrepair, perfect with its ramshackle picket fence and overgrown climbing roses, perfect with the fifty acres that stretched behind it—just enough room for a few cows, a large garden and plenty of space for horseback riding or just walking in their own private pine forest.

Neil settled into his new routine—the courthouse every day, either in Pleasant Gap or one of the adjoining counties that comprised his district, and home every evening—and Ginnie into hers. The newspaper seemed a distant part of her life, missed, but not desperately, and although Pleasant Gap supported a weekly paper, the only contact she had with it was to take out a subscription for mail delivery. Her job now was her home, and for the first time since she'd married Neil, she felt that she truly had a home to care for.

She quickly became a fairly good carpenter—first by watching those they hired for necessary repairs and then by tackling some of the jobs herself—and a wallpaper hanger, and a painter.

The school bus stopped at the driveway each morning at seven-thirty to pick up Todd and deposited him back shortly before four. Neil assigned him responsibilities and, although he carried them out reluctantly, he did eventually carry them out.

Evenings were spent together, and as the days grew longer, more of them were spent outside. Fifty acres, besides being heavenly space, presented an almost unending supply of outdoor jobs, especially because of the state to which the acreage had been allowed to deteriorate. But in the newness of country living, even repairing fence or corrals or dilapidated barn siding became a challenge, not a job, and it was something they were doing together—building with each other, for each other. And when Ginnie and Neil fell into bed at night, sometimes they were so exhausted they could do no more than hold each other. But even with that, they managed to reach a physical closeness that surpassed anything she had ever thought possible.

Ginnie thrived on it. Her complexion glowed, and her eyes sparkled with excitement for each new surprise of each new day. Neil let his hair grow a little longer, still conservative because of his position as a judge, but he made no effort to get to the stylist in Little Rock. And his skin bronzed in the sun, making him even more devastatingly handsome in Ginnie's eyes.

They were still the outsiders in the community, looked upon tolerantly because he was the judge, but with amusement because they were so obviously *city folk*. And now when they went into town on Saturday morning for coffee at the drugstore, they didn't wander absently down the sidewalks or sit in isolation at their booth. There were calls of, "Hi, Judge, how are you? Hello, Mrs. Kendrick, how's that boy of yours getting along? Sure do like what you're doing with that place out there. It's been needing it for a long time."

With the coming of spring, Neil borrowed a garden tiller and dug up an old vegetable plot. Together, they seeded it and weeded it, and when harvesttime came, Ginnie was ready. With the help of her elderly neighbor down the road, a newly purchased pressure cooker and a supply of jars, she learned to preserve her own homegrown produce.

They repaired the picket fence and painted it white, as it should be. The rosebushes leafed out, the house sparkled, and life, for the most part, continued to be wonderful. Just as she had promised. And what wasn't wonderful, would be. Ginnie promised that, too.

Todd still professed to hate the school, small even though it serviced not only Pleasant Gap but a large surrounding rural area. That would change, Ginnie knew, once he made friends, once he felt really accepted. With such happiness and stability around him, how could he fail to be happy?

But he did.

As another winter approached, as evenings grew longer, Todd paced the house or shut himself in his room, refusing to participate in school activities, refusing to try out for athletics, refusing to do anything after class, except to go to the weekend football games.

He wanted a car. That would solve all his problems, he insisted. He was stuck out in the sticks, with no way to do anything unless Ginnie or Neil drove him into town like a baby.

"You're only fifteen, Todd," Neil told him after Ginnie refused to discuss the subject with the boy any longer. "You can't even get a driver's license."

"But you're the judge, Dad. Who's going to hassle me over no license?"

"The answer is no," Neil said firmly. "I don't want to hear any more about it."

And no more was said about it, but when Ginnie walked up from the barn late one afternoon, she discovered both her car and Todd gone. Neil found Todd at a local drive-in restaurant. He left Ginnie's car there temporarily, but he brought his son home.

"I'm not excusing his behavior," Neil told her as he drove her to town to pick up her car, "but maybe you shouldn't have left the keys where they would tempt him."

"In my purse?" Ginnie asked. "In the bedroom?"

And Neil was already so angry, she didn't tell him about the twenty-dollar bill that was also missing. She could be mistaken. She'd thought she'd missed money before, and this time, like the others, she convinced herself that she had probably spent more at the grocery store, or miscounted her change, or forgotten a purchase she had made.

To a degree, she could understand Todd's dissatisfaction with his inactivity. Now that the house was finished, there was little enough to occupy her time in maintaining it, and now that winter was approaching, there was little that she could do outside.

Their social contacts, primarily local attorneys and their wives, provided some outlet for her, but most of the women were deeply involved, either with jobs or with small children. And while Ginnie longed for a child of her own, she knew that Todd was still too insecure in his place in their home to accept another child, yet.

Ginnie became a well-known fixture at the library. She went at least twice a week, borrowing and returning books. But one afternoon, unable to tolerate her inactivity any longer, she dragged her portable typewriter from the back of the closet, remembering with something close to covetousness the sleek little laptop computer she'd left behind when she left her job.

Three weeks later, the efforts of that afternoon appeared in the Sunday edition of the *Arkansas Gazette.* The day after that, the local librarian handed her the feature article, neatly clipped from the newspaper. "Is this you?"

Ginnie nodded, a little embarrassed by this unexpected attention.

"My goodness, I didn't know we had a celebrity in town."

When Ginnie returned to the library Wednesday, she found the clipping tacked to the bulletin board along with a carefully lettered caption, Local Judge's Wife Celebrity In Her Own Right.

"We were thinking of offering a short course in creative writing in conjunction with the junior college," the librarian told her. "I wonder, could we count on you for some help?"

How could Ginnie refuse? There was little enough to do in the way of special activities in Pleasant Gap. She and Neil had discussed that problem. If someone was willing to try to provide an activity, shouldn't she offer what help she could? She agreed, committing herself for six Wednesday evenings, to start the following month.

That Friday, the publisher of the local newspaper called her at home. He offered her a job, which she refused, but she did agree to supply him with occasional features.

And when the PTA heard of Ginnie's efforts with the writing class at the library, she received a call from the organization's president, asking if she would help with the school's program for gifted students. Of course she would, she agreed immediately. And would she chair a committee on the gifted program? Ginnie didn't know if she would be able to handle that, too. But she did.

For Neil, activities crept in as insidiously, becoming involved in the local bar association, and all the local civic clubs. With his position in the community, he found it almost impossible to join one and not the others. Would he teach a class in business law at the junior college? Only two evenings a week?

He was a popular judge, although a newcomer to the area, and although in Little Rock he might have been able to have an unlisted telephone number, he couldn't do so in Pleasant Gap. The people demanded access to their elected officials. Now the nights he was home were often interrupted by the telephone.

And then it was spring again, and time for a garden, time to care for their fifty acres of paradise, and at night when they fell into bed they were often exhausted, too exhausted even to hold each other.

And Todd was sixteen and had his car.

And Ginnie could no longer excuse missing money as a figment of her imagination.

And she could no longer ignore that during the time Todd spent away from the house with his friends, he was probably drinking something stronger than cola.

She didn't have enough experience, then, to recognize red-rimmed eyes and strange speech patterns and the lethargy Todd sometimes evidenced, as being anything but unusual behavior, but she did recognize them for that.

But now, times for discussions of those things with Neil were becoming rarer and more harried. Ginnie was no closer to Todd than she had been the first time she met him four years ago, but there had been a wariness about him then that would not let him expose himself to her. Now he didn't seem to care.

She tried talking to Neil, hesitant conversations in which she suggested that the three of them probably ought to seek the advice of a counselor, but Neil adamantly refused.

"We're a family, Ginnie. We'll keep our problems within our family."

Only when Ginnie found the case of beer hidden in the barn loft did those family problems become serious enough for him to do more than have a talk with Todd.

Neil suspended Todd's driving privileges for a month, increased his household and farm chores and told him to open each can of beer and pour it down the drain.

"But it's not all mine," Todd insisted. "Rick bought it."

Neil glowered at him. "Rick Skelton is only sixteen, too, Todd. How did he get it?"

When Todd claimed ignorance, Neil picked up the kitchen phone and dialed the Skelton residence.

"Hello, Jim," he said to Rick's father. "This is Neil Kendrick. We have a problem out here I thought you ought to be aware of. We found a case of beer in the loft, and Todd tells me that at least part of it belongs to Rick. You don't mind if we go ahead and dispose of it, do you?" After a moment of silence, he continued. "No. I don't have the answer to that yet, but I think you and I probably ought to see what we can find out."

Todd raged at his father for betraying him with a friend, but it was Ginnie for whom he held his anger, Ginnie who had really betrayed him, Ginnie who bore the brunt of his anger in his cold silences, his ignoring her requests and eventually her demands. Ginnie, the outsider. And he renewed his efforts to make her feel that way.

When she arrived home from the grocery store one afternoon and found a familiar nosed-down, paint-battered car in the driveway, and Tommy and Joe and Barry in the living room, she experienced a strong sense of déjà vu, knowing full well what caused it, and an even stronger premonition.

They met her at the front door, on their way out as she came in.

"I'm going running around. You weren't home. Dad said I could." Todd spoke belligerently, almost as though he dared her to tell him that he couldn't leave.

Angry? Yes, Ginnie was angry. Hurt. And frightened. Her life was beginning to replay those last miserable months in Little Rock, and she didn't know what to do about it.

Neil's announcement that night after dinner didn't help any, either. He followed her into the kitchen, nursing a cup of coffee.

"Ginnie?"

She looked up from the pan she was scrubbing.

"This term of office expires next January. I have to make a decision about whether we're going to stay in Pleasant Gap or not."

She put down the pan and turned to face him. "We aren't going back to Little Rock, are we?"

"I don't know," he said. "But if we decide to stay, I'm going to have to be reelected to keep this job. I'm going to have to campaign. What kinds of problems is that going to cause?"

Another election. She'd known it was inevitable, but when they first came to Pleasant Gap, it had seemed so far away she'd managed not to think about it. Now it seemed that she must. And yet, even another campaign was preferable to returning to the city. There, she'd lose Neil forever. She knew that with a certainty. Here, it would only be for a short while.

"I understand."

"You always *understand*, Ginnie. I need more of an answer than that."

"We can't go back, Neil. Todd—"

"Todd hates it here," he interrupted.

"I know. But it's better for him in Pleasant Gap than it would be in Little Rock."

"Is it, Ginnie?" Neil set down the cup and hesitated before he spoke. "I hadn't meant to have this discussion tonight, but maybe it's for the best. I wanted to give Todd what I didn't have. I wanted to give him a home, and a childhood, and a family. I wanted him away from the influences that had infiltrated the city's schools. But I'm not sure it's working.

"Can't you accept that he's just a boy? A boy who has been through more than most adults could tolerate. You're the grown-up, Ginnie. Can't you find some way to get through to him? Or have you given up?"

She had wanted to talk to him about Todd, but this was not at all the conversation she had envisioned. The unfairness of it sharpened her words. "Can't *I* find some way to get through to him?"

All of the hurt of the afternoon came flooding back. "Do you suppose that I haven't tried? And what do I get in response, Neil? At best, a sullen lack of cooperation. I've asked that we seek help, because I don't know what to do anymore."

"Maybe if you accepted the fact that he is only sixteen, that he has interests that are different from yours, that he has friends that you won't necessarily approve of—"

"Who—Tommy Wilcox?" she interrupted. "Is that what this is all about? That must have been some phone call this afternoon. You're right! I don't like Tommy Wilcox. I think he's a mean little sneak. He's much too old for Todd to be running around with, and God knows what he's involved with. He was trouble before we left Little Rock, and he's worse trouble now."

"How, Ginnie?" Neil's tone cross-examined her. "Is it because of something you know about Tommy Wilcox? Or do you just not like him? Be honest about it, not emotional. Let the facts, not your imagination, control this discussion."

"Imagination. You think it's my imagination? All right, let's don't talk about Tommy. Let's talk about Todd. Here are the facts. He is sullen, resentful, personally sloppy. He neglects his responsibilities. He has been drinking—we found the beer in the loft. Money has disappeared on a regular basis from my purse. He has little respect for other people's property. He has no respect for other people's feelings."

These things had been bottled up inside her for so long that she was beyond controlling the way they came out.

"I think he has a serious problem, Neil—more than just adolescence, more than just a hurt, lonely childhood, more than just adjusting to a new town. I think he has a real problem, and I think he needs help. And I know that I need help to cope with him."

She saw in his stance and in his eyes the expression that had quelled many a witness. "Do you even try to cope with him anymore?"

"Oh, what's the use!" Ginnie cried. "He's your son, and you should be protective of him. But you should also look at him with some of the same skepticism you show me. I'm your *wife,* Neil. Don't you think it's time you started placing some value on what I tell you?"

"Maybe I would, Ginnie, if you could ever present me with a calm, dispassionate view, but it's difficult to place much credence on accusations made in the heat of anger."

"You aren't blind, Neil. Don't act like you are. Surely you can see what's been going on."

"What I can see," he said, "is that this house has become a war zone, just like the one we left in Little Rock, and I don't like it."

And though he couldn't bring himself to say the words, not yet, please not ever, Neil didn't like facing the fact that this last year and a half might have been a mistake, that they had torn up their lives and lived a fool's dream for nothing. He didn't like acknowledging that Ginnie could possibly be right about Todd. He wouldn't, couldn't acknowledge that Todd needed professional help.

"He's an angry boy who needs love and understanding, Ginnie."

"He's *had* love and understanding, Neil, but at some point he has to begin to be responsible for his own actions. We can't go through the rest of our lives excusing his behavior because of what happened to him as a child."

"But did you ever excuse it for that reason?" He didn't mean that. He remembered the look on her face the night they had returned from their honeymoon, the first time Todd had snubbed her. He'd seen that look again, too often. He'd seen it recently. He saw it now.

He didn't want her hurt. God! Surely there was something she could do. His talking with Todd did no good. Todd never railed against Ginnie. All he ever said was, Ginnie doesn't like me, she doesn't trust me, she doesn't want me here. And while Neil didn't believe that of her, he couldn't convince Todd of the truth.

"Have I ever excused him because of that?" How could Neil even ask? "Constantly, Neil. Constantly. From the first words he said to me in private."

Ginnie caught back a sob as she remembered the pain. "Do you know what they were? I never told you about that, did I? The first words your son said to me in private the night we returned from Galveston—I tried to talk to him about his mother, to tell him that I didn't intend to force my way into her place. What he said was... what he said was, 'Maybe you'll die, too.' But that won't be necessary, will it? All I have to do to make him happy is pack my suitcase and leave. So don't talk to me about excusing his behavior because of what he's been through."

Her words chilled him. *No!* She had misunderstood, or blown Todd's comment out of proportion.

"Why would he want you to leave?"

"I don't know." She was quieter now. Reflective. Subdued. "At first I thought it was so he could have you to himself. Now I wonder if it isn't so that there will be no one who notices what he's doing, who disapproves of what he's doing."

"Ginnie, you act as if he's some sort of criminal and I condone his actions."

"No. You don't condone them. You just aren't aware of them."

"And why is that?" he asked. "I'm not imperceptive."

"No, Neil, you're not imperceptive. Just absent."

There. It was out again. He'd known it would come out, and if she resented his absences now, the campaign would only make things worse. But, damn it, what did she expect of him? He'd twisted his whole life around for her and still she wasn't satisfied, still she wasn't able—or willing—to make an effort to meet him. There was just so much he could do. He'd sacrificed his career plans, he'd sacrificed his law practice,

and now it seemed that she wanted him to throw his
son at a psychiatrist and wash his hands of him, too.

"You say he wants you to go, Ginnie. He says that
you want him gone. That you don't like him, you
don't trust him, and you don't want him here."

"God, Neil." She sagged against the cabinet. "How
did we get to this point? He said that I don't like him.
Do you know how much I wanted to love your son,
how much I *want* to love him, but he throws all my
affection back in my face.

"No. I don't trust him. I want to. Each time I think
I might be able to, something else happens.

"And as for wanting him gone..." She sighed. She
couldn't lie about this anymore, not even to herself.
"Yes. Sometimes I think our life would be much easier if we didn't have to contend with him. Sometimes
I wish to God his mother were still alive so we could
send him to her for at least a summer, so we could
have time to ourselves."

She saw a betraying muscle twitching in his jaw.

"But that doesn't mean that I want him gone."

"You wish his mother were still alive?"

Ginnie nodded, warned to silence by the chill in
Neil's voice.

"And if she were, you'd ship him off to her? Like a
piece of baggage?"

"No. Not like a piece of baggage. Like a son visit-
ing his natural parent!"

"A natural parent who never wanted him. That was
the problem, Ginnie. The only reason Ann fought for
custody of him was to thwart me, and she *did* treat
him like a piece of baggage. She never had time for
him. She was always too busy with her men and her—
her drinking and her trips to Vegas and her pills. If she

had cared for him, do you think she would have committed suicide in the house, leaving him, a child, to find his mother's body?''

"Oh, sweet Jesus," she moaned. "You never told me that."

"And you never asked. You never asked one thing about Ann. You never asked one thing about Todd's life with her."

Neil turned from her, crashing his fist futilely against the kitchen table. And he had never told her. She'd always seemed too innocent, too fragile, to expose her to the sordid details of his first marriage and of Ann's troubled life. So what did he do? He hurled those details at her in the middle of an argument.

"Neil—I—" Ginnie's voice was stricken. He tensed at her tentative touch on his shoulder. "I'll try," she promised. Her voice broke. "I'll try."

She did try. In the face of Todd's increasing belligerence, Ginnie exerted what she felt was superhuman effort to be understanding. In spite of Tommy's weekly visits and Todd's long absences from home, she continued to try. And if custodial care was the only thing Todd would allow, she swore she would give him the best custodial care she could. Gran had set an example for her a long time before. It was the only one Ginnie knew to follow. But clean laundry and home-cooked meals were things he accepted carelessly as due him, while the affection she offered he just as carelessly rejected.

Todd still pushed past her to leave the room. The first time he actually made physical contact with her while going by her, Ginnie attributed to an accident. His shoulder brushed hers as he passed, causing her to step back, off balance. He was angry and defensive because she had been questioning him about his actions. Surely, though, it had been an accident.

The second time, he'd been acting strangely—drunk, almost, although she detected no smell of alcohol about him.

"What's the matter, Todd?" she asked, concerned. "Are you ill?"

"Oh, shut up!" he yelled at her.

And this time when he pushed, it was with his hand, not his shoulder, and this time there was no way she could delude herself into believing it was an accident.

"You're always after me about something. Just leave me alone. Just leave me the hell alone!" he shouted as he stormed out of the house.

Imagination? she asked herself. Emotion?

"Neil," she said late that night as she lay in the dark on her side of the bed. "I'm worried about Todd."

Neil tensed at the beginning of the familiar litany. What had she concocted now?

"I think..." She hesitated, unsure of how to continue, because these were only thoughts, impressions, and she had no proof. "I think he's—taking something."

Neil expelled his breath. First it was a psychological problem. Now it was a chemical one. Well, why should Todd be exempt from her rationalizations? She'd blamed all the other problems of their marriage on outside forces. Outside forces somehow seemed easier for her to cope with.

"Go to sleep, Ginnie."

"I'm serious about this," she persisted. "He's acting more strangely every day."

"So it has to be dope? Did you think that would get my attention, knowing how I feel about the stuff? Leave him alone, Ginnie. For God's sake, just leave the boy alone and let him grow up."

He heard her sharp intake of breath and knew full well that she would be crying silently. So she was hurt again. Once he'd have done anything he could to see that she didn't hurt. Now—now pain seemed to have become a way of life. For both of them.

He stared with hollow eyes at the shadows on the ceiling. So Todd was acting strangely. Well, he couldn't blame him. The battle lines were drawn so firmly in this house they were almost visible. Todd tore at him constantly now. The boy was troubled. He couldn't ignore that any longer. There was a lot of Ann in Todd.

But, God, there was a lot of him in Todd, too. Looking at Todd was like looking in a mirror, or looking at a picture of his own father. He understood his son's insecurity. He'd felt it himself. And he knew, but didn't know how to stop the fact, that Todd's life was repeating his own frustrated, lonely early years.

Neil's father had left him to his own devices most of his childhood, only taking an interest when Neil strayed too far from accepted behavior. And in spite of the move to Pleasant Gap, that's what Neil was doing to Todd. Ginnie could have helped. Why in the hell didn't she see that she could have helped?

But he wouldn't abdicate. Not the way his father had.

No. He couldn't blame all of Todd's problems on Ann. A lot of them had to come from this house. And from him. But he was frustrated in his inability to act, except in anger.

Just like his father, Neil realized with a jolt of fear. Just like his father, who had spent the last years of his life paralyzed by indecision, going through the motions of life but unable to act on anything unless forced to, until one day he refused to be forced into action any longer. A heart attack was listed as the official cause of death, but Neil knew better. The man had decided not to hurt anymore. When he was not a great deal older than Neil was now, he had gotten up one morning, sat in his favorite chair and willed himself to die. Neil knew that, without question.

He felt Ginnie shifting on the other side of the bed, turning away from him, with unspoken censure in her actions and an unspoken sense of betrayal in her tension. He knew that he had disappointed her, that he constantly disappointed her now, but, God, he couldn't be strong for them all, not much longer. And yet, what right did he have to expect strength from Ginnie? At least not strength enough for him to draw from.

Still, if she would just once turn to him at night, if she would just once comfort *him*. He almost reached for her to draw her into his arms, to take from her the comfort she seemed incapable of giving, to lose himself in the pretense that things were the way they once had been.

He heard a strangled sob break from her. Even loving her, those damned tears would still be sliding down her cheeks. Even loving her, he'd not be able to get away from this awful, crushing sense of failure.

He turned on his side, away from her, and some time later, much later, he finally slept.

Ginnie could no longer pretend. The house, once her haven, daily more resembled an armed camp. Each of them seemed to be waiting for the other to say something, to do something that would propel them into the final cataclysmic scene. And it would be final. She knew that. For that reason, she edged around any possible conflict, drawing into a shell, trying not to see, trying not to hear, trying not to feel.

And the final scene, when it came, came with such devastating fury that it was months before she could even bring herself to think about it.

Ginnie was in the kitchen making piecrusts—Happy Homemaker, she thought, at least in appearances—must keep up appearances—when Todd came in through the back door. She glanced up at him. He didn't speak. He just went directly through the kitchen. She shrugged but didn't speak, either. A short time later, he appeared with an armload of jeans and underwear.

"These didn't get washed."

"They weren't in the hamper," she said patiently. "I've told you, I won't dig through your room looking for your laundry."

"I don't have anything clean." He extended them toward her. "And Dad wants me at the courthouse this afternoon."

She put down the rolling pin, lifted the fragile dough and began fitting it into the pie pan. "I've shown you how to operate the washing machine, Todd. Now might be a good time to put that knowledge to work."

He looked at her for long, angry moments before dropping the armload of laundry onto the table, onto her piecrust.

"Damn you, Todd!" The words erupted from her before she could think not to say them.

His expression closed in a way so similar to Neil's that she caught herself, biting back more angry words.

"I didn't mean that," she said, shamed by her outburst.

"You meant it, all right. You just didn't go far enough. When are you going to ask him to make a decision, Ginnie? Isn't that what it's coming down to? Well, I'll tell you, if my father has to choose between me and you, you won't be the one who stays."

She fumbled for the clothes, gathered them in her arms, and, unable to face him, she whirled and went into the laundry room, threw the clothes in the washing machine not bothering to sort them, dumped in detergent and spun the controls.

When she returned to the kitchen, Todd was no longer there, but she heard him in the house, and later she heard the front door slam as she dumped piecrust and unrolled dough into the trash. She washed the residue of flour from her hands and reached for her wedding ring, which she had placed in a small dish beside the sink. It wasn't there, and her heart thudded sickeningly as she looked at the empty dish. She lifted the dish to look beneath it, but she knew it wouldn't be there. Before starting to work on the crusts, she had carefully placed the ring in the decorative dish she kept beside the sink for that very purpose. She had not moved it, and no one had been in the kitchen except her... and Todd.

She ran for the front door, reaching it just as she heard his tires squealing as he spun out of the driveway. "Oh— Oh— Damn it!" She beat her palm against the door. "How could he? How could he?"

Without stopping to think, she ran down the hall, slamming open his door as she burst into his room. He'd just hidden it, she thought. Not even Todd would take her wedding ring not meaning to return it.

Since childhood, Todd had kept special treasures in his desk, demanding utmost privacy. Ginnie never opened his desk drawers. Now she did, rummaging through them, searching frantically, one drawer, two, three, the cubbyholes in the writing top.

She didn't find the ring. What she found were almost illegible scribblings on sketches of such violence she threw them from her in horror. What she found were packages of cigarette papers. What she found was a jeweler's box she had thought long ago lost filled with small, round, green seeds.

Todd's dresser drawers came next. In the bottom one, under his winter sweaters, she found a velvet bag that had once encased a bottle of whiskey now full of change, half dollars, quarters and a wallet bulging with paper money.

What she found on the top shelf of his closet was a plastic bag from a bookstore in Little Rock, and inside that bag, not marijuana as she had half feared, but a rainbow assortment of pills in various plastic pockets.

What she found was confirmation of all her accusations, of all her fears, and, God, she wished she hadn't found that. But she didn't find her ring.

She carried the money and the bag of pills back into the kitchen and collapsed in a chair. God, oh, God, what did she do now? This would kill Neil. And yet he had to know.

She shook her head from side to side as if denying what lay on the table before her. A picture of a twelve-year-old Todd playing with Charlie floated through her mind. "Oh, Todd," she moaned.

She knew Neil's schedule. He had pretrial conferences slated all morning. He'd be closeted with attorneys and case files and other people's problems until at least noon.

Ginnie threw her head back and closed her eyes. If ever anything qualified as an emergency, this was it, and yet she couldn't bring herself to disturb him, not yet. She sat there in stunned silence, her mind unable to grasp the full implications of what lay on the table, and watched the face of the clock across the room, watched the hands move around it, approaching noon, bringing the moment of confrontation closer, and closer.

She swallowed convulsively. It was almost time. If she didn't call soon, she wouldn't be able to reach him until after lunch.

The chair scraped across the floor as she pulled herself to her feet. Old. She felt ancient as she dialed the number, as she explained to Neil's secretary that she didn't want to interrupt him but that it was important, that it was *vital,* that he come home during the noon recess.

The sound of tires in the driveway assaulted her ears as she replaced the receiver. Hastily, she grabbed the contraband, stuffed it into a lower cabinet behind some bakeware and slammed the cabinet door shut. One packet had fallen to the floor. She snatched it up just as Todd entered the kitchen.

"I need my clothes."

"Clothes?" she asked numbly, not remembering for a moment the washer full of laundry.

She told herself later that if she had been more attuned to him, she would have understood why he paced so restlessly, why his hands moved with quick, uncoordinated jerks, why his glance darted from object to object, why his words came so rapidly, but at that time she didn't.

"And I need my wedding ring."

"So?"

"So give it to me, Todd. Before this situation gets any worse."

"What if I said I don't have it?"

"I wouldn't believe you. I don't believe you. What I don't know is why you took it, but I want it now."

He grinned at her, a malicious little grin that only twisted his mouth, and thrust his hand into his pocket. He pulled out the ring and held it between his thumb and forefinger, turning it in the light.

"What are you going to do? Tell Dad?"

"Probably." She held out her hand. "Give it to me."

He tossed it into the air and snatched it back in one quick motion. "I think you lost it, Ginnie. I think you lost it and you want to put the blame on me."

Suddenly, fear, like nausea, rose in her throat, but she couldn't let Todd see that. He was, after all, still a boy. He was, after all, still under her care. She swallowed her fear and stood upright. Never raising her voice, never taking her eyes from his, she again extended her hand. "Give me the ring."

"He won't believe you, you know. Why would I want to take your wedding ring?"

She still held the packet of pills in her other hand. "I don't know, Todd," she said, "but then, why would you want to take these?" She held the pills so that he could see them.

"You sneak!" His words exploded into the room. "You've gone through my things! How dare you go through my things? Give me those!"

He grabbed for the packet, but she drew her hand back, shaking her head as she inched away from him to the safety of a stance behind the table.

"You want the ring?" he yelled. "I'll give you the ring. But you give me those pills. You had no right to go in my room! All you ever do is meddle in my life!"

He calmed, suddenly and deceptively, and a note of cunning crept into his voice. "The ring for the package, Ginnie."

She sighed and shook her head. "That's a poor trade, Todd. Don't you mean the package and my silence? I won't be blackmailed into it."

She saw the rage in his eyes then and knew that she should never have confronted him alone. She tried to maintain a facade of bravery, a facade of control, but it was too late. He sensed her fear and with that knowledge he became bolder. He smiled, a mindless smile she knew she would remember in the dark of night as long as she lived, a smile that told her wordlessly that he would take the package from her.

"Stop right were you are," she said.

"The package, Ginnie."

"It won't do you any good, Todd. It's too late."

"Give it to me!" he screamed as he lunged across the table, grabbing her wrist. She twisted away from him, but her foot caught in the chair leg. Falling, she was falling. She tried to balance herself, but he still held her arm. She cried out as she felt the edge of the table bite into her cheek, and then she was under the table, scrambling away from him. He caught her ankles, pulling her out from under the table, fighting to reach her hand. She dropped the packet. It wasn't worth it.

"Stop it, Todd. You've got to stop it."

But he didn't stop. Now he was no longer reaching for the package, just hitting at her blindly.

"You had no right to do that!" he insisted. "You had no right to do that! You had no right to do that!"

She tried to fend off his blows, not wanting to hit him, not wanting to hurt him. Lord, how could she make him stop? She caught her fist in his hair and yanked violently. Off balance already, he tumbled to the floor beside her, still flailing, still yelling. She used the second she had to strengthen her grip and twisted around behind him with her fingers at his scalp, clutching his hair, holding her arm stiff to put as much distance as possible between her and his vicious fists.

"Be quiet!" she yelled at him, clenching her hand against his scalp. "And be still!"

Could she hold him? She didn't know, but she couldn't let him go. He tried to twist around, and she yanked again at his hair.

"I said, be still."

Her breath came in ragged gasps. If she dared let go, could she make it out the back door before he reached her? What would happen if he broke loose? What in God's name was she doing in a mess like this? And where was Neil? She glanced at the clock. It was after twelve. He should be free by now. *Please don't let him go to lunch before he comes home,* she prayed.

"We're getting up, Todd," she said. "Just don't try anything funny, or I'll snatch every hair you've got out of your head."

She rose awkwardly to her feet, never loosening her death grip, or her life grip, she thought frantically, and then tugged at his scalp until he clambered to his feet. Taller than she, he could easily have reached her had she not held him from behind, and easily overpowered her had she not held him off balance with his head tugged back. She edged her way backward, toward the telephone, leading him in an ungainly shuffle. She cradled the receiver under her chin and then, unwilling to take her eyes from him for even one moment, dialed the operator and asked her to place the call to Neil's office.

Her legs trembled. She hoped that Todd couldn't feel the tremble in the hand that held him. Please, she prayed silently as the telephone rang, and rang, and rang. The back door opened, and Neil walked through, stopped with his hand on the doorknob, and looked in stunned disbelief at the scene in front of him.

"Oh, thank God," Ginnie moaned, relinquishing her hold on Todd's hair and collapsing against the wall. The forgotten phone slid from her shoulder and dangled at the end of its cord, the persistent noise of the other phone ringing the only sound in the room. "Thank God."

Chapter 7

The litter on the kitchen table told the story as the two of them sat in subdued silence. In addition to the money and the pills, even the drawings from Todd's desk, there were also the contents of his pockets—his car keys, a list of telephone numbers, and, of course, her wedding ring. Neil's face was ashen in the harsh light of the kitchen. For the first time, Ginnie noticed that strands of silver had crept into the dark hair at his temples.

He looked—old, she thought in amazement. As old as she felt. And—broken.

Todd had been banished to his room. Ginnie didn't know what reaction she'd expected from Neil, what punishment she'd thought he would mete out, but it had to have been more than his cold, clipped command to Todd to go to his room, to stay there until and *if* he ever told him it was all right to come out.

Neil glanced up at her as though seeing her for the first time. "You have blood on your cheek," he said woodenly. Not, she thought, My God, you've been hurt. Not, Ginnie, I'm sorry. Not, Can I do anything for you. Just—You have blood on your cheek.

Stiffly, she rose from her chair. Now that the adrenaline had finally stopped its frantic pumping, she was aware of the mass of aches that covered her body. She walked to the sink, tore a paper towel from the rack, wet it with cold water and winced at the sting its contact with her face caused. Surprisingly, there were no tears. It was as though she had finally gone way past the point where tears could bring relief.

"What are we going to do?" she asked.

Neil watched the paper towel on her cheek, but he wasn't seeing it, she knew. He was looking far beyond her.

"I don't know."

"Neil, I—"

"I don't know, Ginnie. God, I never would have believed . . ." His words trailed off. He ran his hands through the loose packets of pills on the table, sifted his fingers through them, and then dropped his hand. "It's easy to be objective when it's someone else's life," he said finally. "I know what ought to be done. I ought to turn this over to the authorities. I ought to help find his connection."

He turned to her as though pleading for understanding. "But I can't do that Ginnie. I can't turn him over to the courts. What I'm probably going to do is pollute our septic tank with this. But what am I going to do about Todd?"

He turned bleak eyes toward her. "And what am I going to do about you? I had no idea . . . You told me, but I didn't, couldn't believe the animosity ran so deeply. There isn't any hope, is there?"

She remembered the rage in Todd's eyes and the hatred in his voice. She shook her head slowly, dragging it back and forth. "I don't think so."

"Then it's over."

Funny, had she always known it would come to this? It seemed she must have, because his words held no surprise for her.

"I can't leave him in the same house with you anymore, Ginnie. He was high today. I don't think he would have...done what he did had he not been high, but I can't guarantee that he won't ever be high again, and I can't guarantee that once having done what he's done..." He paused and pushed his hand through his hair. "I can't guarantee that it won't happen again."

Todd, she heard. Todd, Todd, Todd. Not her. Not her fear. Just Todd. *If my father has to choose between me and you, you won't be the one who stays...* Had she always known that, too? She nibbled on her lower lip, not even able to lash out in her pain. "I'll leave, of course."

Unable to look at him any longer, she glanced out the window at the lengthening shadows through the trees in their pleasant backyard, at Charlie stretched out and dozing in one lingering patch of sunlight. In their misery, the afternoon had passed unnoticed. Evening fast approached. "Should I go now?"

"No. Not tonight," Neil said. "He's finally come down. He'll sleep for hours."

Not, Ginnie, I don't want you to go. Not—she laughed soundlessly and mirthlessly—of course not. She couldn't expect that Neil would throw his sixteen-year-old son out in the street, not for her, not for anyone. And she wouldn't let him, even if by some miracle he offered her that choice.

"Tomorrow, then," she said. There was defeat in her voice but no bitterness. "Tomorrow."

Neil watched silently the next morning as Ginnie finished packing her suitcases, taking only clothes, her ancient typewriter and a few personal things. She snapped the latches on the last case, straightened and eased her upper back against the aches and bruises that had stiffened her muscles.

"Where will you go?" Neil asked.

"I don't know. I'll let you know."

They faced each other in awkward silence. Neil thanked his years of courtroom experience for the control that let him keep all expression from his face and from his voice, for the control that kept him from crying out his rage and his frustration, the control that kept him from begging Ginnie to stay with him, from swearing he would keep her safe and damn the consequences.

But he couldn't do that. Not to her. Not to Todd. Not even to himself.

"Is Todd awake yet?" she asked.

Neil nodded.

"I have to say goodbye to him."

Yes. He recognized now that she would have to do that. And all it had taken was the ruin of three lives for him to gain such clarity of vision. He stepped aside to let her pass.

Ginnie paused outside Todd's door. She would be justified in leaving without saying anything to him. She knew that. But she had to make one last effort.

She knocked on the door but entered without waiting for his call.

Todd sat propped on his unmade bed, wearing the same clothes he had worn the day before, with his stereo earphones clamped securely in place. The power light on the stereo told her it was on.

"What do you want?" he asked.

She signaled for him to remove the earphones. He groaned but did so, and from the discarded phones across the room, she heard the raucous sounds of a screaming rock band.

"I'm leaving, Todd."

He shrugged.

"I just wanted to tell you—" God, this was harder than she thought it would be. "I just wanted to tell you that, even though you don't believe it now, I always wanted to love you. I always wanted us to be a real family. I always wanted you to care for me."

He half turned from her.

"No, Todd. Listen to me. I'm leaving, but I'm not giving up. I love your father, and I'll be there for him if he ever needs me. And I'll be there for you if you ever need me, Todd. Remember that. Please."

He snorted in disgust, grabbed the earphones and clamped them back on his head, turning from her, dismissing her. She stood for a moment in indecision, wanting to shake him, wanting to make him listen, wanting to make him acknowledge what she had said. Finally, though, she turned and left the room.

Neil carried her suitcases out to the car and put them in the trunk. He did not open the car door for her. She stood beside it. There was so much she wanted to say to him, too, but she couldn't. Not now.

She opened the door and slid into the seat. He still watched. When she backed from the driveway, she paused in the road long enough to turn and look at him. He was still watching her, unmoving.

Ginnie drove aimlessly, for truly she had no place to go, and slowly, because truly she didn't want to leave. About half an hour out of town, she realized that the road was taking her back to Little Rock. Habit, she supposed. There was nothing for her there. Her home was in these hills, not in the concrete and asphalt of the city.

She pulled off onto the shoulder of the road and sat there. Her home was in these hills. Her home was with Neil. She still loved him, although she had not told him that. Why had she endured the agony of the last years only to turn tail and run, now, to give up, to admit defeat? Their biggest problem was their constant struggle over Todd. Maybe she couldn't live in the same house with him anymore, but she could be close to him. She could provide a place for him to get away from Todd. She could at least be close to him.

They had come to Pleasant Gap to save their marriage. Maybe they still could—not in an orthodox manner, but maybe there was still a way.

She waited for a break in traffic, made a U-turn and headed north, back to Pleasant Gap. She stopped at the library. She and the librarian had become fairly close over the last few months. The librarian's maiden aunt had died earlier that year, willing her a fully furnished home. It was a risk, Ginnie knew, and there would be talk, but she had to try.

"Have you sold your aunt's house yet?" Ginnie asked.

"Not yet. You know what the real-estate market is these days. Why? Do you have a buyer in mind?"

"Not really. What I'd like to do is..." Nothing in her life had been easy. Why should this be any different? She'd already acknowledged her failure to herself. Now she was about to admit it to someone else. "What I'd like to do is rent it."

Neil visited once, hesitant, almost embarrassed. And a second time, less so but still uneasy. There seemed little to say once past, How are you? How is Todd? Little, that is, that Ginnie was capable of saying.

She confronted the publisher of the paper to see if his offer of a job was still open. It was. She agreed to take it until the end of the summer.

She heard of an opening at the junior college and applied for it, not knowing whether she would actually be there when school started. And she waited.

When Neil's telephone call came one afternoon just as she walked in the front door, she clutched the receiver and sat down at the small federal-style desk in surprise.

"Ginnie, I have to tell you something. Could we—"

A knock on the door distracted her, for no one ever knocked on her door.

"Just a minute, Neil," she said. "There's someone here."

"No. Wait, Ginnie. I—"

"It won't take a second." She propped the receiver on the desk, letting herself wonder for a moment why he seemed so reluctant for her to answer the door—

Todd? But she'd left the door unlocked when she ran to answer the telephone. She had to go.

A young deputy sheriff stood outside her screen door, neatly starched and pressed, and obviously uncomfortable with what he had come to do. "Mrs. Kendrick, ma'am? I'm real sorry." He thrust folded papers into her hand and hastily retreated to his marked car.

Ginnie unfolded the papers and stared at them until comprehension soaked through her numbed senses. A complaint in divorce. Neil had filed for divorce. Neil was divorcing her....

She walked back to the desk. The receiver scraped as she picked it up. "Ginnie?" She heard his voice, tinny and distant. Carefully, very carefully, she hung up the telephone.

The next week Neil and Todd were gone. A new judge was appointed to fill out the term. Neil's opponent in the election was assured of a noncontested victory. And a For Sale sign graced the picket fence of the house in the country.

Later, much later, when she could bear to, she drove past the house that had been their hope for the future. The roses splashed a riot of color across the fence. She looked at it through blurred eyes. "The American dream," she said bitterly. "A place in the country. My God, even the white picket fence." Angrily, she shifted into gear and drove away. She would not return.

September arrived, along with classrooms full of scrub-faced youngsters who, if they had any problem other than receiving their financial aid, Ginnie tried not to know. In addition to her journalism classes, Ginnie also sponsored the school newspaper. Al-

though no longer a member of the PTA, she continued in an advisory capacity with the gifted program,
and with the various special programs sponsored by
the library.

She was still identified as Judge Kendrick's wife, or
Todd Kendrick's mother, and she supposed that in a
small town that would always be the way it was. One
day when a young man at the hardware store said,
"Oh, I know who you are," she steeled herself for the
inevitable. "You're the creative-writing lady from the
library. I want to tell you how much my brother enjoyed that course last year. That was all he could talk
about for weeks."

She smiled as a thrill of the first genuine pleasure
she had felt in months ran through her. At long last
she had an identity of her own. She engaged in animated conversation with the young man for several
minutes, giving him the dates of the next short course
and eliciting a promise that he would enroll in that
one.

And sometime during those months, she learned
that it was all right to do things for herself because she
wanted to.

And sometime during those months, she learned
that she didn't have to be dependent upon another
person for her own happiness.

And sometime during those months, she began,
once again, or maybe for the first time, to enjoy a life
she made for herself.

The ache was still there. It surfaced every time
someone asked, "How's the judge getting along?" or
"How's Todd? Haven't seen him in ages." But she
knew that those questions would be a part of her life

for as long as anyone remembered that she'd once been Neil's wife. The ache was...bearable.

And sometime during those months, the students in her classes became individuals, not just her nine o'clock journalism class, not just the staff of the newspaper, but Scott and Ken and Marsha, individuals who enriched her life, who responded to the affection she allowed to surface.

And sometime during those months, she discovered the peace Gran had known from her church. The first time Ginnie visited the tiny rock building that housed the church, it was late in an afternoon when she thought she couldn't possibly drag herself through another day. She'd slipped into the church, to a back pew, pulled down the kneeler, and then, feeling somehow as though she had no right to be there, just sat in there for fifteen, twenty minutes, half an hour, until the serenity of the cool quietness, the dark wood, and the paintings worked its way into the corners of her soul. Soundlessly, she slipped to her knees. She hurt. She hurt so bad. "Please," she prayed. Just the one word. "Please."

Decorations in one corner at the back of the church announced that there would be a young people's folk Mass the following Sunday. She'd be there. She wouldn't promise more than that one Sunday, but she would be there for that.

So her life went on. Funny, but she hadn't thought it would. And it went on...well. There was a fullness to it she had never expected. And while the eight-page college newspaper wasn't the *Arkansas Gazette,* she derived a great sense of accomplishment from it. And while the students in her classes weren't her own children, she derived a great deal of pleasure from them.

And while the tiny house she still rented from the librarian wasn't the home she'd always envisioned, it welcomed her each evening when she returned to it.

Only at night did memories of her past intrude. Ginnie told herself that in time those, too, would pass, but as the months spun by, they didn't. Sometimes— sometimes they didn't intrude on her presleep musings. Sometimes they waited until she dozed off and then haunted her dreams. Sometimes she awoke and the scent of Neil, the touch of Neil, the taste of Neil were so real that she moaned and clutched her pillow to her. But the memories would pass, she told herself. If she told herself that often enough, maybe eventually she would believe it.

She almost did believe it, until the day she walked from the newsroom with Marsha, the student editor that fall, laughing with her over the mistake the typesetter had made and they had, fortunately, caught in time, and saw Neil leaning against her car.

A pickup truck roared to a stop in front of them. Marsha's boyfriend, a redheaded, freckle-faced, irrepressible clown, waved at them. Laughing, Marsha hurried to join him, leaving Ginnie alone on the sidewalk.

Mechanically, her legs moved, carrying her to her car, and while her legs moved woodenly, reluctantly, her mind raced. What did Neil want? Why did he have to come back? God, he looked awful. There was more gray in his hair now. Was he sleeping enough? Did he miss her the way she missed him?

Neil didn't smile. He didn't speak. He waited for her. She wondered fleetingly if the same turmoil of thoughts racing through her mind could be troubling him, too.

She paused in front of him. "Hello, Neil." Her words gave no indication of the trip-hammer action of her heart.

"Are you through for the day?"

She nodded.

"Could we talk?"

Was that wise? Hadn't they said all that needed to be said? What could rehashing old problems do except bring alive the hurt?

"We—" Her voice failed her. She tried again. "Do we have anything to discuss?"

Only a clenching of his fist betrayed that he felt any emotion. "I hope so," he said finally. "Can we go to your house?"

She couldn't be alone with him, not in the privacy of that little house, not without saying things that ought not be said. Not without listening to what her traitorous body was already telling her.

"I don't think so," she said. Some place public would be much safer, and yet just seeing him had brought all the memories to life. Some place public would not do, either. She'd embarrass them both by breaking down. "What about the park?"

"All right. Shall we leave your car here?"

Even the closeness in a car was too much for her to face right now. "No. I'll meet you there."

The park, deserted and bare in the winter, greeted them much as it had that first time. The same squirrel, or perhaps a well-trained descendant, chattered at them. The same bench waited for them.

Neil looked around distractedly. "It was a long time ago, wasn't it?"

She knew without asking that he was referring to their first visit to the park. "A lifetime."

"How are you, Ginnie?"

"I'm all right, Neil. I'm making it . . . all right."

Silence clamped its wedge between them.

"And you? How are you, Neil?"

"I miss you like crazy."

No! Even as she thrilled at the words, her mind screamed, *No! Not now! Not again!* "I'm sorry," she said. "How's Todd?"

His expression closed, but whether in acknowledging the shift in conversation or the subject it had followed, she couldn't tell.

"Irritating. Belligerent. Personally sloppy. Let's see if I can think of some of the other things you tried to tell me about him. Most of them still apply."

"And the drugs?"

"I don't think so. If he's doing anything now, he's keeping it well hidden."

"And his temper?"

"God, Ginnie, I didn't expect a miracle. And there hasn't been one."

"How are you, Neil?" she asked again, softly.

"All right, I suppose. I've gone back into practice with Kirk. Business is good."

"It would be," she told him. "You always were a fantastic lawyer."

And then, relenting at the bleak look on his face, she admitted. "I've missed you, too."

He sighed and sank back against the bench. "Is there anything we can do?" he asked.

She leaned back, too, staring across the empty park toward the same tree he was staring at. Neither of them saw it. "I don't think so. Nothing's really changed, has it?"

His answer was less than a whisper in the chill afternoon air. "No."

He stood up abruptly. "I know you must be busy. I won't keep you any longer."

She rose to her feet awkwardly. Side by side, not touching, they walked back to where their cars were parked. She reached for her door handle.

"Ginnie?"

Her throat tightened on a sob she refused to let him hear as she turned to him. His arms lifted hesitantly.

"Oh, Neil." She leaned against him, letting his arms enfold her, sliding her own arms around him and hugging him close. They held each other for countless moments, knowing the embrace was not enough, yet fearing anything deeper.

Finally, she pushed away from him and attempted a smile. She failed at that. "Take care of yourself," she said.

He nodded. "You, too." He opened her car door for her. Wordlessly, she got in and drove away.

No, the memories hadn't disappeared yet. But they would. There were no other options. Time healed everything. That's what she told herself. It always had. It would. It did. Except for the aching loneliness.

Except for the fear and then the anger she felt when Todd began periodic visits to his friends in Pleasant Gap. Ginnie never saw him on the streets or heard of one of his visits that a cold knot didn't form in her throat. This was her home now, and while he never personally accosted her, she considered his trips intrusions into her territory, intrusions into her life. "You ruined my life once before," she raged impotently, alone in her house, clutching at anger to stave off a fear that, no matter how often she told herself was probably unnecessary, refused to release her. "Stay out of it now."

The glimpses that she caught of him told her that not only had he ruined her life, he was well on the way to ruining his. Older now, larger, he'd be at least his father's height, maybe taller by the time he stopped growing. There was a difference in those familiar features, though, a sallowness of skin, a slackness of muscle, a vacantness sometimes in his eyes, and a puffiness about his face, which sent a feeling of vague dread through her. She didn't understand it, but she didn't want to get near enough to examine it.

When she received the telephone call late one night, she was stunned but not surprised.

She struggled up from her dream, fumbling in the dark for the jangling instrument.

"Ginnie?"

Neil's voice, weary beyond description, floated with the dream voices in her mind.

"What's wrong?"

"It's Todd," he said. "I just wanted you to know..." He paused as though searching for any other words. "I just wanted you to know that you were right."

"What's happened?" She was awake now, her nerves screaming, her mind attuned to the defeat in his voice.

"He—he got hold of something. We don't know what yet. We had to subdue him. He's in Children's Hospital. Apparently, he's going to be all right physically, but I've arranged to have him committed for—for at least a thirty-day observation."

Ginnie sat upright, holding the receiver and herself tightly, protectively.

"Neil, are *you* all right?"

"Me? Yeah." He laughed humorlessly. "I'm fine, Ginnie. I'm--strong. I . . . I just thought you ought to know. I'm sorry I woke you."

"No. That's all right. Neil?" But she heard only the sound of the dial tone.

"Take care of yourself," she whispered into the dark.

A week and a half later on a Friday night, at 8:17, as shown by the regulator clock hanging beside her front door, Todd showed up. Ragged, dirty, terrified, he opened the screen and banged on the wooden door until she answered it.

"Help me, Ginnie, you've got to help me," he gasped and collapsed in the doorway.

The door shoved against her hands. She couldn't close it, not with him blocking it, but she couldn't open it, either. Could she?

Ginnie knelt on her side of the door, reaching to touch Todd's shoulder. He grabbed her wrist.

"Don't let them get me please don't let them take me back . . . Dad did it he hates me Ginnie don't make me go."

"Ssh, Todd. Ssh." She soothed him as she would a frightened child. "I'm not going to hurt you. Nobody's going to hurt you."

She helped him to his feet and then, because there was nothing else she could do—she couldn't just push him out in the yard and slam the door on him—she helped him into the house. What was he doing here? Why wasn't he in Children's Hospital? She settled him on the couch, but he didn't release her.

"Please Ginnie they do awful things to you there."

His face was puffy, puffier than she had ever seen it, and the vacant look was back in his eyes. His hysteria grew as he held on to her.

"It's all right, Todd," she crooned. "Everything is all right. Just relax. Just relax."

"You won't let them take me away?"

She couldn't lie to him, but she couldn't leave him in the grip of fear, either. "I won't let anyone hurt you, Todd. You're safe now."

She smoothed the dark hair away from his forehead. "Now you're safe, Todd." She stroked his forehead and murmured to him until she felt his hand slide from her wrist, until she recognized the even breathing that told her he had either fallen asleep or passed out—she didn't know which. She eased herself from the couch and went into the bedroom, tripping the pitiful excuse for a lock as she closed the door.

She dialed Neil's office number, because it was the only number she had, and on the fifth ring, an impersonal female voice answered.

"I'm sorry, Mr. Kendrick is out of town. He won't be back for several days." And then, probably because the woman had recognized the near hysteria in Ginnie's voice, she added gently, "In cases of emergency, he's asked that his calls be referred to Mr. Williams. Shall I ask him to return your call?"

"No!" Ginnie couldn't take the chance of a ringing telephone awakening Todd. "No. I'll call Kirk."

Kirk didn't believe in unlisted telephone numbers. At least she could find his home number through directory assistance. Thank God, he was home.

"Kirk, I have to find Neil."

Kirk obviously heard the same thing the woman at the answering service had heard. "What is it, Ginnie? What's wrong?"

"It's Todd. He's here."

"There?"

"Yes. He showed up just a few minutes ago. Kirk, there's something terribly wrong with him."

"Oh, good God. How did he get out?"

"What do you mean, *How did he get out?* Didn't they let him out?"

"Ginnie, he's got another twenty days of observation. There's no way they would have released him. Not with Neil out of town."

"Lord, where is Neil? I've got to reach him."

"You can't. I sent him up to my cabin in the mountains. There's no phone up there, Ginnie. There's no way to get in touch with him unless I send the sheriff out there to look for him. Which I will do. Just as soon as we take care of this emergency. Where is Todd now?"

"He's asleep. At least I think he is. On the couch."

"Can you get out of the house?"

"What—I—yes. I think I can. What? Kirk, what's going on?"

"Didn't Neil tell you?"

"Only that he'd—I can't remember what he actually told me and what I think I heard. I think he said— I think he said that Todd had taken an overdose of something, that he'd had to be subdued, that Todd was physically all right but that he was going to stay in the hospital for observation."

"He didn't tell you why Todd had to be subdued?"

"No."

"Ginnie, he tried to kill Neil."

"Oh, my God." Every sound in the house was suddenly amplified, every creak, every groan, every brush of every branch against the outside walls. Ginnie clutched the receiver in one hand, watching the door as if she expected Todd to burst through at any moment. "Oh, God, Kirk, what do I do?"

"You have to contact the police, Ginnie. And you have to get out of that house. Is there a back door?"

"Yes, but I have to go through the living room to get to it, too."

"Don't do it. Go out a window if you have to, but get out of there. I'll call the hospital here and tell them where Todd is."

"But he's—" She remembered Todd's pleading. "He's frightened, Kirk. He's like a little boy. He's not violent now."

"Ginnie, get out of the house. Ginnie, do what I tell you and get out of that house."

She didn't argue any longer. As quietly as she could, she eased open a bedroom window, snatched her purse from the nightstand and slid out into the night, feeling like a burglar.

She put her car in neutral and coasted out of the driveway, not attempting to start the engine until she was in the street. Then, blindly and frantically, acting on emotion only, she drove to the sheriff's office.

The night dispatcher recognized her and smiled as she walked into the office, then frowned when he noticed her obvious agitation.

"What's wrong, Mrs. Kendrick?"

"Todd," she said. "Todd's at my house."

If anything, his frown deepened as his face evidenced his confusion.

"He's—he's escaped from the psychiatric ward at Children's Hospital. He's quiet now, but he can be dangerous."

"Let me call the judge."

She hadn't expected this response, yet she knew the judge he meant was Neil and knew this man would seek Neil's permission before doing anything.

"You can't reach him," she told the deputy. "I've tried. He's off camping somewhere."

The deputy scrubbed at the back of his neck with a large hand. "Do you have copies of the commitment papers, or any kind of a court order?"

"No." Would this scene have played out any differently in a large city? Or was it just in this insulated community where, in spite of all the months when she thought she'd been building her own identity, she was once again thrust back in the role of the judge's wife— the judge's discarded wife?

"I talked to Neil's law partner tonight. Kirk said— Kirk said that he would contact the hospital. They'll be getting in touch with you. You've got to go get Todd. You've got to do something. I can't go back there."

"I can see you're frightened, Mrs. Kendrick, but understand my position. I can't just go out and pick him up on your say-so for being in your house. You raised the boy, ma'am. What'll the judge say if I haul his son off to jail?"

The phone buzzed persistently, and the deputy grabbed for it, not quite able to hide his relief at this distraction. "Sheriff's office. Yes. Yes." He glanced at her. "That's right. Will do."

He replaced the receiver and touched the microphone. "Unit seven." Ginnie heard the garbled response. "We have an escaped mental patient." Ginnie sagged in relief. "Meet a party at—" He glanced up at her.

"It's 105 Chandler."

"Meet a party at 105 Chandler. Unit eleven?" Again came an unintelligible reply. "Can you back him up?"

The radio squawked again before the deputy turned toward her. "I'm sorry, Mrs. Kendrick. Will you be all right?"

"Sure," she said, breathing deeply. How could she say anything else? "Sure."

She met the officers at her house. Fortunately, they came silently, with no screaming sirens, no flashing blue lights to alert Todd, to alert the neighborhood. There was no visible drama.

Ginnie opened the front door and let them into the house. One reached for his gun, but she shook her head violently. Todd was still asleep on the couch, innocent in repose. Should she be the one to wake him? She started toward him. One of the officers stopped her with a hand on her shoulder. "Is he dangerous?"

"He can be."

"Then let us do this. You stand back."

Carefully, both deputies approached the couch. One gingerly took Todd's wrist and eased a handcuff around it. Equally gingerly, he reached for the other wrist and snapped the other cuff into place over it, too.

Todd stirred, stretching out his arms. When he met with resistance, his eyes opened. He looked at the officers, at the cuffs, and finally at Ginnie.

Not hysterical now, not violent, Todd spoke with a calm that terrified her as yelling would not have, as screaming would not have.

"You did this."

"Come on, Todd." An officer reached for him.

Todd shook away from him and stood up. He lurched toward Ginnie but was caught by two pairs of strong arms.

"I'll get you for this. Sometime when you least expect it, I'll be back. I'll tear you up, Ginnie. You won't get away with this."

Only when they reached the door did he revert to his hysteria. "No!" he cried, a long, agonizing scream, as he fought his restraint.

Ginnie could still hear him screaming as they thrust him into the back seat of the patrol car.

Chapter 8

How long had she gripped the table? Slowly, Ginnie became aware of the ache in her fingers, which still held the other edge, the smoothness of the wood beneath her cheek, the inanely tinkling music-box Christmas carols floating in from the living room.

And how long had she lived with the terror of Todd's threat? Weeks, actively. Months, on a less intense level. But not since she'd bought this house had Ginnie consciously remembered his words, and that had been well over a year and a half ago.

She roused herself. She couldn't stay like this all night. Already her body protested the unaccustomed posture. She sat up, easing her shoulders and rubbing a hand across the back of her neck. She no longer heard ice pelting against the window. Had it stopped?

She lifted her head to look outside and froze in stop action. A shadow. Just the corner of a shadow, outlined briefly as it passed the kitchen window. Had someone been watching her?

The roar of her heart drowned out all other sounds as she tried to listen for anything unfamiliar. Was that a footstep? Or just another creaking timber in this old house?

A footstep. She heard it again. Another. Then another. Approaching the back door. And then the crash of a fist on wood. And another. And another.

She sat there, still frozen in immobility.

"Ginnie! Ginnie! Are you all right?"

Neil. She loosed her tightly held breath. Neil.

The chair scraped across the floor as she willed her knees to straighten, as she willed her muscles to relax, and then fell with a crash as she willed herself to stand up.

"Ginnie! Open this door!"

She fumbled with the lock, and when she had unfastened it, the door thrust open in her hands.

"Are you all right? I—"

"I—you frightened me."

"I'm sorry. I've been pounding on your front door for— When you didn't answer, I came around the back. I saw you through the window. I thought..."

Ginnie backed away from the door, letting him enter, and righted the overturned chair. He closed the door behind him.

They stood in awkward silence. She knew what he must have thought, seeing her stretched out across the kitchen table.

He looked older, she thought. Strands of silver now liberally laced the dark hair at his temples. The lines running to each side of his mouth were deeper, as though he seldom smiled anymore. If anything, though, he was more handsome than the laughing, triumphant young lawyer she had fallen in love with. And more—more foreboding than she had ever thought possible. He was the man she had lived with, the man with whom she had gone through so much, and yet he was a stranger.

"No. I'm . . . I'm all right," she told him.

A sharp pain of desire twisted through Neil. Ginnie could still do that to him. After all these years, she still held that power over him. And yet she looked as vulnerable and as innocent as the day they met. Only now, her eyes held thinly veiled fear and a wariness that he knew he was responsible for putting there.

"Have you heard—" They spoke simultaneously. Both fell silent.

"How are—" Their words mingled again.

"Please," Ginnie said. How on earth did she greet an ex-husband in the middle of the night, one whom she had never wanted to leave, one whom even now she wanted to take her in his arms, to hold her, to tell her everything was going to be all right?

"Won't you sit down?" she asked, wanting to say more, knowing she couldn't. "You must be cold. Can I—can I get you something hot to drink?"

Neil seemed to rouse himself and stamped the snow from his shoes on the doormat. "Yes. That would be nice, thank you. Let me use the telephone to call the sheriff's office."

"It's . . ." She gestured ineffectually toward the telephone. "It may be out. It was giving me trouble earlier. I don't know if—"

"Your telephone is out of order?"

She recoiled from the harshness in his voice.

"It does that sometimes in wet weather. The telephone company promised they had finally fixed it the last time. I think the problem must be in the connection at the back of the house, but I'm not sure."

He muttered an oath. "When did it start acting up?"

"A little while after you called the last time."

He lifted the receiver and scowled before slamming it back in place.

"Damn, Ginnie! What would you have done if—" He bit off his words. "I have a phone in my car. Can I go out the front? It will be easier than walking through the drifts out back."

"Of course." She led him through the house, let him out the front door and stood shivering against the cold in the open doorway waiting for him. He returned with a garment bag and a shaving kit.

"I've given everyone the mobile phone number, and the sheriff's office is going to try to roust out an emergency crew for your telephone. There hasn't been any word yet." He indicated the garment bag. "Do you mind if I change? I got wet wading through your backyard."

Only then did she realize how he was dressed. A black cashmere overcoat covered a smartly tailored black suit showing just a hint of silk in the fine wool blend. White-on-white silk shirt. The gold studs and cuff links she had given him for Christmas the first year. Black tie, of course.

"I did interrupt your party. I'm sorry. Was it terribly awkward for you?"

He glanced at her, raking his eyes over the floor-length emerald wool she wore. "It seems that mine wasn't the only party interrupted tonight, Ginnie.

Don't worry about it." He shifted the bag in his hand. "Where can I change?"

She showed him to the guest room, got him hangers for his clothes and fresh towels for the adjoining bath, and retreated from the room, back to the safety of the kitchen.

As she measured tea and poured boiling water into the pot, she heard the faint sound of the shower running. A hot shower, she knew, to chase away the chill. At one time, she would have carried his cup into the bathroom to him and held it outside the shower curtain waiting for him to reach for it. She'd never had the nerve to draw back the curtain and blatantly watch him, and now, for one mad moment, she felt an impulse to do just that.

Stop it, Ginnie! she warned herself. She'd been afraid to do that when she'd had the right to. Now she no longer had that right.

When Neil returned to the kitchen a few minutes later, he wore jeans, a rust-colored turtleneck sweater that set off the breadth of his shoulders and black socks.

"I left my boots in the car," he said by way of apology. "If you don't mind, I won't go out for them now."

Aren't we formal? she thought. Two strangers skirting the edges of what they really wanted to say. At least she was. Maybe he wasn't. Maybe he had no more to say than what he already had.

She handed him his tea. When he said thank you in that same restrained voice, she could stand it no longer.

"Are we going to avoid the subject all night?"

Neil glanced at her sharply, drank from his tea and set the cup on the counter. "Only if you insist upon it."

He overpowered her. Just by standing there in his sock-covered feet, his presence threw her so emotionally off balance she felt incapable of beginning the conversation. Already her familiar red and white kitchen was alien territory, not hers any longer, indelibly marked by him.

She picked up her cup. "Let's go into the living room." There, perhaps, she wouldn't feel so confronted by him, as though, somehow, this were all her fault.

But there, on the sofa, lay the disarray of pictures and papers just as she had left them. Ginnie felt Neil watching her as she scraped them, and her wedding ring, into the wooden box and set it on a side table.

The fire had burned down to coals, but the tree lights still twinkled, the puppy still slept in his box and the music still repeated itself. The room was the same as it had been hours before, but now, with Neil here, it would never be the same again. She silenced the stereo.

Neil knelt by the puppy, watching it but not disturbing it, and then, to give himself something to do, he added logs to the glowing embers. This room, he thought, like the rest of the house he had seen so far, was much like Ginnie. It had a gentility, an old-world quality which should be spared the harsh realities of the present. The physical symbols of security with which she had surrounded herself didn't make saying what he had to say any easier.

"Your house is—is very comfortable," he told her, postponing the inevitable conversation.

She didn't acknowledge his comment. She sat silently. Waiting.

He straightened and looked into the fire. He might as well get it over with. There'd be no better time.

"Todd has been under heavy medication for the last two years." He spoke haltingly. "It seemed the only way of controlling him. The doctors are pretty sure that his first big flare-up was caused by angel dust, PCP, but whether he took it deliberately or had some slipped to him, we'll probably never know. And he has some flashbacks because of that. But that isn't the whole of it, Ginnie.

"He's a seriously disturbed boy and probably has been for years, at least in varying stages. Recently, a new psychiatrist joined the staff at the hospital. Some of these medications they give are pretty awful in and of themselves and over a period of years can mask the underlying symptoms to a degree that the doctors can't get a true picture of the patient's progress.

"What they were doing was weaning Todd from all medication."

Neil turned to her. No. There would never be a better time to say this, or a good way. "More or less to see what's left of him, I think, although that wasn't the explanation they gave me."

He drew a steadying breath, looking away from the shock and compassion he saw in Ginnie's eyes. Continue, he told himself. Get it over with.

"Todd has had a couple of flare-ups since the change in his medication, but when I visited him this morning, he seemed quiet. He seemed almost rational. We talked about Christmas. He asked when he could come home. The hospital tells me that nothing unusual happened the rest of the day, that he went to bed quietly, that he seemed to be looking forward to Christmas morning."

"Do they know when he left?" she asked. "Or how?"

"It isn't a jail, although there is pretty strong security there. Apparently, he forced a lock in the reception area. For some reason, the alarm didn't go off. He went through a window. They found a piece of his shirt hanging from the top of the gate."

Ginnie sank onto the edge of the couch. "Why, Neil?"

If he heard her underlying question, he ignored it.

"By the time he shows up, or is found, he may not even remember why."

Neil turned his back to the fire, standing motionlessly in front of it.

"You don't really have any reason to worry, Ginnie. He can't get far in this snow." His voice dropped—low, so low. "And the authorities in at least four counties are looking for him."

The magnitude of that struck her. These would be strangers looking for an escaped mental patient, not men who had known Todd most of his life. The night that Todd had shown up at her house, one of them had even attempted to draw a weapon on him. Unbidden, Neil's story of Mickey Flannagan flashed through her mind. She choked back a sob.

"Oh, God. Will they hurt him, Neil? I never wanted him to be hurt."

She looked up at him, her eyes pleading with him to tell her that nothing more tragic would happen. He heard the question in the tremor of her voice and saw it in her eyes, but he couldn't give her the answer she wanted, that *he* wanted.

"I don't know, Ginnie. I hope to God it doesn't come to that."

She caught her breath on a sob. She would not cry. Now was not the time for tears. What must Neil be going through? It had to be much worse for him than for her. Now she *would* be strong. She could give him that much, if nothing else.

She watched wordlessly as he walked toward her. He knelt beside her and placed one hand on her shoulder.

"It will be all right, Ginnie."

She heard no conviction in his words. Tentatively, she reached out to him, tracing the lines of care in his face. The sob broke from her as he gathered her to him, cradling her against his chest.

"Ssh, Ginnie. It will be all right. It will be all right. Please, God, it will be all right."

"What have we done?" she moaned, holding him to her, needing him to deny her question and knowing he couldn't. "Oh, Neil, what have we done?"

Ginnie felt the softness of fine wool beneath her cheek, the ridge of an arm beneath her back, a hand draped possessively over her breast and another resting gently on the swell of her hip. *Neil,* she thought contentedly and snuggled more closely against his sleeping warmth. *Neil?* Her eyes flew open.

Light flooded through the sheer curtains. A bright chill pervaded the room. They lay entwined on the sofa. Ginnie shifted uncertainly, and, as she did, she felt the change in Neil's heartbeat that told her he was also awake.

She felt his arm tighten and his hand move slowly, reluctantly, from her breast to the relative safety of her ribs.

She looked up at him and saw in the depths of his dark satin brown eyes, unguarded now, a desire as great as that which sparked to life within her, and she became aware that his were not the only arms, the only hands, that had trespassed during the night. Her own were around him, not so intimately, but speaking just as eloquently of her own unconscious needs that sleep had freed her to express.

She should move, she told herself. She should end this embrace of body and of eyes, but she was incapable of doing that.

Without tightening his clasp, he held her. Without speaking, he spoke to her. She knew that with one sign from her, or perhaps without it, Neil would kiss her, and that if he once kissed her, they would not stop until they had brought to fruition the intimacies they had so innocently started. So long as she didn't move. So long as she didn't break the spell.

She waited, her throat dry, her heart pounding frantically, her eyes never leaving Neil's face. She felt the slight tremor that moved over him. Then he was bending, slowly and oh, so carefully toward her, until his mouth was just inches from hers, and then less than a heartbeat away. He hesitated, his lips parted slightly. His arms tightened around her.

Yes, Neil, she pleaded silently. Yes. They could worry about the consequences later, so long as they had this time, now, just for the two of them.

She moistened her lips and wondered if she would dare rise to meet him if he did not end this agonizing anticipation.

An irritating buzz grated across her nerves. Neil's head jerked toward the noise. The spell was broken.

Ginnie sagged in disappointment against him. "My alarm clock," she said without waiting for his question. "I forgot that I set it."

She scrambled from his arms and into her bedroom. Grimacing, she slapped off the alarm. "Traitor," she snapped. "You never sound nearly that loud or commanding when I need you to."

She debated returning to the living room. No. The moment was gone. Anything between them now would probably be as forced as the conversation had been last night.

Instead, she retreated to her bathroom. A bath, quick and functional, was what she needed now, and warm, serviceable clothes. And her boots, if she could just remember where she'd put them the last time she wore them.

When Ginnie emerged later, neatly armored, her wayward thoughts and emotions tucked inside her as far as possible, she found the front door open. The storm door barred most of the chill and let in the clear, cleansing light. A trail of footprints led from the porch to Neil's car, on down to the street to the newspaper-delivery tube, and back to the house. Other than that, and a small turmoil of disturbed snow in front of his car, the yard was an unmarred blanket of glistening white. Neil's black dress shoes, wet again, sat neatly on the doormat in the front hall.

She became aware of the aromas of coffee and bacon and smiled. Neil had always been a breakfast person. She made her way into the kitchen, stopping only to check on the puppy. His basket was empty.

She found the puppy in the kitchen, trying with his ungainly little legs to keep up with Neil's long strides. Neil didn't seem to be paying much attention to the collie, but he stepped carefully over and around him as he made his way from the stove to the refrigerator to the table, preparing breakfast with a skill which surprised her. He had never before been even competent in the kitchen.

"I plugged in the pot. Your coffee is on the table," he said as he noticed her. He turned back to the stove. "Eggs? Or do you still prefer to skip those in the morning?"

"Just bacon and toast," she said. "Thanks."

So. They were back to being polite strangers. And yet, she realized, not quite.

She noticed a bath towel draped over the back of one of the kitchen chairs and a few lingering drops of moisture on the collie's coat. "You took him out?"

"Mmm." Neil's response was muffled as he busied himself with the eggs. He slid them onto one of two waiting plates before he carried both plates to the table. "He didn't quite know how to handle snow. I'm afraid he mostly played. He's going to have to go back out."

He motioned toward the table. "Your breakfast is getting cold."

The table was set properly. The toast was just the right color, not burned as she'd half expected. The bacon was crisp, just the way she liked it. His eggs were the way he had always requested them and even she had trouble preparing.

"You've acquired a new talent," she said as she sat down.

"Survival," he said. "One learns to survive."

And then, if he'd meant anything deeper than the words implied, he hid it well as he occupied himself with the mechanics of eating.

Ginnie sat silently, trying not to watch Neil and unable not to. It was Christmas morning, they were involved in a drama that few people could even imagine, and yet they sat across the table from each other like any couple, on any morning. The only thing that would make this ritual more routine would be for Neil to pick up the folded newspaper lying on the edge of the table and hide himself behind it as he finished his coffee. He didn't do that.

"It looks as though you have a feast prepared and waiting in the refrigerator, Ginnie."

Her attention jerked back to the present. She had forgotten all about today's plans.

"Do you need to get ready for company, or finish dinner, or..." He hesitated. "Do you want me to disappear for a while?"

"No, I—no. Dinner isn't until this evening, and it isn't here. I do need to take the food I have prepared out to Cassie and Frank's sometime this afternoon, though, and I should call Cassie and tell her that I won't be there for dinner."

She started to rise to go to the telephone but remembered its wet-weather vacation. "I don't suppose the phone's dried out enough to be working yet, has it?"

"No. I tried it earlier. I checked on the repair crew when I called the sheriff this morning, but it's anybody's guess when they'll get here. Ice took a whole section of line down south of town. They'll have to finish up there before they can even look at your problem."

"It will probably cure itself before then," she said, attempting lightness. "Sunshine always helps." She sobered. "Has there been any word?"

"No." Neil frowned and peered at her over the edge of his coffee cup. "What do you mean, let them know that you won't be there?"

"Well, it's just that, with things the way they are, I..."

"It's Christmas Day, Ginnie."

"Yes," she said softly. "It is."

"And from the looks of the contents of your refrigerator, you've put a great deal of planning into this dinner."

"Yes. I have."

"Then go. If something happens, I can get in touch with you."

"And leave you here?" she asked. "Alone?" She shook her head. "Oh, no. I'll go, but only if you come with me."

"Ginnie, be reasonable."

"I am being reasonable. If I were at your home, would you leave me to wait alone?"

"These are your friends. Do I even know them?"

"It doesn't make any difference," she said. "Neil, it's Christmas Day. No one needs to be alone on Christmas Day." She reached for his hand where it rested on the table, but stopped before she touched him as one clear, whimpering thought made itself heard.

Todd is alone on Christmas Day.

She picked up the plates, almost angrily, carried them to the counter and set them down beside the sink.

"Leave those for now?" Neil asked softly.

"But, I—" She turned to him and found a whimsical smile softening features that had become too stern, too harsh.

"It's beautiful outside, Ginnie. The puppy needs to go back out. Besides, I want to explore that enormous old backyard of yours in the daylight."

And Ginnie did something she had never done before. She left dirty dishes waiting in her kitchen.

"All right," she said, drawn irresistibly to his smile. "Let's get our coats."

Outside, a winter wonderland awaited them, unbroken white except for tiny twiglike prints that covered the mound of snow that was her birdbath, and miniature craters and scratches showing where seed had fallen from the feeders.

They paused on the back steps. She was reluctant to mar the purity of the snow. "It looks almost gift-wrapped," Ginnie said reverently.

The collie, however, was not hesitant. He plunged off the step into a drift and whimpered his shock.

Neil laughed and bent to retrieve him. "Watch out, little fellow. You're going to have to learn what you can and can't do."

He lifted the pup and placed him farther over, where the drift was not so high, where the snow only scraped the puppy's belly.

"Have you named him yet?"

"No. I've been waiting for a name to attach to him, but the one that keeps recurring is Charlie."

"Funny. That's what I was thinking. He reminds me so much of Charlie when he was a pup. I really miss that old dog. Even at the last, when he was almost completely helpless, I kept remembering him as he had been when he was young." He straightened and brushed his wet hands on his thighs. "Well, something will come to you."

"Yes." She blinked back unexpected moisture. Dogs couldn't live forever. Charlie had been old when she and Neil married. "Yes, I suppose so."

She stepped off the porch into the snow. The first step was the hardest, she realized. She shook her head. Good grief. She was only thinking about walking in the snow.

Ginnie strode to the birdbath, making plowing tracks as she went. She'd intended only to brush the accumulation of snow from the top of it, but she turned and looked back toward the house where Neil teased the pup. Without stopping to think, she scraped up a handful of snow, packed it and sent it sailing toward his broad back.

"What!" he yelped, and then turned in her direction. A diabolic grin lit his face. "You want to play rough, do you?"

He scooped up a double handful, packing it as he advanced on her.

"No, Neil. Wait a minute," she said, laughing, backing away from him.

Splat! The snowball hit her squarely on the left shoulder.

"You rat," she cried. But she had just as good an aim as he. Besides, he was much closer now.

His midsection received her second snowball. She ducked. His second only grazed the top of her head. Then she was laughing and running, and he was chasing her. She circled the birdbath once, twice, and started back toward the safety of the house. She almost made it, but Neil caught her with a flying tackle to her ankles just before she reached the back steps.

Ginnie went down with a whoosh and rolled over, still laughing, scooping snow as she turned, and flinging it at him. And then the three of them were on the ground together: she, Neil and the puppy. Neil caught her arms in one hand, holding them above her head, laughing and threatening her with a handful of snow. She kicked out playfully, and he trapped her leg with his.

And suddenly there was no more laughter.

Ginnie's breath caught and refused to move. The sound of her heartbeat was the only sound she heard. Neil's breath, visible in the chill, hung suspended between them, as did time.

The blare of a car horn, a long, drawn-out, demanding summons from the front of the house cut through their isolation. Concern, fear almost, replaced the desire in Neil's eyes.

"Who is it?" she asked.

Neil released her and scampered to his feet, holding his hand out to her. "It's my telephone. It's wired to the horn."

She waved his hand away. "Go on. Hurry and answer it. I'll follow you."

For a second, he looked as though he would insist on helping her, but the horn blared again, and he turned, running toward the sound.

Ginnie pushed herself up off the ground and gathered the puppy to her. Not running; no, for she very much feared she didn't want to hear the news this telephone call would bring, she followed Neil's footsteps through the snow.

He had yanked open the driver's-side door and now perched half in, half out of the car as he held the receiver of the console-mounted mobile phone to his ear, frowning. Ginnie stopped at the front of the car. Wet, now, cold, and apprehensive, she stood there hesitantly. Neil looked up just as she shivered, and he motioned for her to go into the house.

Feeling very much the coward for leaving him, she did so, anyway. She went through the motions of drying the puppy, removing her wet boots, changing into dry jeans and socks, and still Neil remained outside. She glanced out once. He continued to hold the receiver and appeared to be deep in conversation with someone.

He entered the kitchen just as she finished filling the sink with hot, sudsy water, and had begun stacking dishes in it. She'd required more activity than merely piling dirty dishes in a dishwasher and pushing a button.

"Where's your broom?" he asked.

"In the pantry." Ginnie nodded toward the pantry door. "Why?

Neil opened the pantry and dragged out the broom. "I'm going to see if knocking the snow off that connection will help your telephone."

She followed him onto the back porch, lifting first one sock-clad foot, then the other, away from the cold of the wood as she watched him batting at the snow that covered the telephone junction box.

"Neil, what is it?"

"Go on back in the house, Ginnie. It's too cold for you to be out here without any shoes on."

"And it's too cold for you to be out here in wet clothes playing telephone lineman. What's going on?"

Neil sighed. He reversed the broom and swept the last of the snow from the connection. Only then did he join her on the porch. "Come on," he said, and abruptly ushered her into the house.

"Rumor. Rumor is what it is, Ginnie. Just rumor."

"Do they know where he is?"

Neil shook his head, breathing deeply. "Everyone seems to know where Todd is. Only it's always in a different place. He's been reported as far west as Russellville, as far east as Memphis, and as far north as Searcy."

"So no one really knows."

"No."

Ginnie took the broom from him. "Go change into some dry clothes," she said. "I'll listen for your car horn."

"And for anything else?"

She nodded. "And for anything else."

"All right." But before he left the room, Neil reached behind him and threw the lock on the door.

Chapter 9

Early that afternoon, while Neil had the puppy outside, Ginnie again tried the telephone. Neil's efforts and several hours of bright sunshine had repaired the problem, as she had known they would. She dialed Cassie's number.

"Thank goodness," Cassie said, laughing. "I was beginning to get worried. I've been trying to call you off and on since early this morning. The phone just kept ringing and ringing and ringing. Did you get the telephone-company repair crew out there today?"

"Are you kidding?" Ginnie asked.

"Well, never mind. It's too nice a day to get into that discussion again. Listen. Father McIntyre is going to be able to come to dinner, after all."

"Great," Ginnie said.

"Well, maybe not so great," Cassie corrected. "He has to leave early. What I was trying to call you about was to ask you if you'd mind coming out late this afternoon instead of waiting until tonight. Say, three? Maybe three-thirty?"

"Of course, except—" Ginnie glanced out the window, toward Neil.

"Except what, Ginnie?"

"Can you make room for one more person?"

"Of course," Cassie said. "Don't tell me you have—be still my heart—a date?"

"Not exactly. Neil is here."

"Neil?" Cassie asked. "Oops. Me and my blasted big mouth. Neil? Your ex?"

"Yes."

After a moment of silence, Cassie asked suspiciously, "Does this have anything to do with that telephone call you got last night? Are you all right, Ginnie?"

"Oh, yes. Yes. It's—look, Neil's coming back toward the house now. I can't really go into it, but there's a problem with Todd—"

"His son?"

"Yes. I promise I'll explain, but I need to bring Neil with me. Is that okay?"

"Of course it's okay, you idiot," she chided gently.

"Thanks, Cassie."

"Oh, and by the way," Cassie added, "come casual. You don't want to have to trek up to the house in fancy clothes. There's no way you can get up the driveway in your car."

Neil, surprisingly, did not object to using her car or to letting her drive. She gave him Cassie's telephone number so that he could leave word where they could be reached, and he helped her carry the food to her car.

"It's practical," he said later, when they were almost at their destination, "but why on earth did you buy a four-wheel drive?"

"Because it *is* practical," Ginnie told him as she turned the serviceable vehicle off the highway and onto an unpaved road. "Because with it, I can do things like this, or even go off the road. I love these mountains, and this vehicle just helps me to see more of them."

The roads really weren't as bad as she'd expected. There had been a little thawing during the day, but, so far, not enough to turn the roads into the almost impassable mud they would be later. However, she didn't attempt Cassie's driveway—not because she thought the Bronco couldn't make it, but because the top of it was blocked by an enormous snowman.

Ginnie laughed and parked the car at the base of the hill. "I hope they've got pictures of that," she said as she reached for a bag of food. "Are you ready to climb the hill?"

Neil glanced around at the snow-shrouded pines and at the road that ended with this driveway. "They believed in getting away from it all, didn't they?" he asked as he reached for the other bag.

"Just another pair of transplanted city folks," she said and then stopped abruptly. She'd been about to compare Cassie and Frank's need for solitude with their own earlier quest.

She'd already told Neil that Frank taught English at the college, that Cassie had interrupted her own teaching career to raise their sons, that they'd been in the area for less than two years and that they attended the same church as she did. There seemed nothing else to say. They trudged up the hill in silence, concentrating on the icy path.

Inside the gaily decorated house, chaos reigned, audible even from the front steps. Cassie opened the door for them and, rather than unload the bags into her arms, they carried them into the kitchen before divesting themselves of their coats. There could have been an awkward silence as Ginnie introduced Neil to Cassie, but Frank walked into the kitchen, followed by Father McIntyre, and the moment passed in only slightly stilted first words.

From the den came the muted sounds of a televised football game and the excited voices of three boys.

Frank laughed. "I hope you're a football fan," he said to Neil. "We need another adult to even things up in there."

"I am," Neil admitted, laughing, but he looked questioningly at Ginnie. She smiled at him, nodded and took his coat.

Cassie remained quiet while they put away the coats, even while they unloaded the food from the bags and placed it in the refrigerator, in the oven or on the counter to wait for a last-minute warm-up in the microwave. When the telephone rang and Ginnie jumped, Cassie shot her a sharp look before answering it. She spoke briefly before going into the den, with Ginnie following. Neil, already looking toward the kitchen, waited, Ginnie knew, to be summoned.

However, it was not to him that Cassie spoke.

"Father McIntyre, the parish secretary is on the phone. Would you like to take the call in our room?"

"Yes, thank you, Cassandra. Please excuse me," he said to the others.

Neil eased back into his chair, and Ginnie returned quickly to the kitchen.

"All right," Cassie said when she joined her there. "What did you think the call was about? And don't tell me *nothing,* because I saw the look on your face and on Neil's."

Ginnie sagged against the cabinet. "You don't know about Todd," she said.

"No. What about Todd?"

"It all happened before you came to Pleasant Gap."

How could she start to explain something that had no explanation? By cutting through to the heart of it immediately, Ginnie decided.

"Todd has been in a private sanitarium for over two years. He's under court commitment, although they have allowed private care. The last time he came to Pleasant Gap, he promised to... He promised to hurt me. Last night, he escaped."

"Oh, Lord." Cassie leaned back against the feast-laden counter, watching her friend, listening but not questioning except with her eyes.

"We believe he's on his way to Pleasant Gap."

"Then that call last night...?"

"Was from Todd."

"Oh, Ginnie, why didn't you say something then? You—you could have come here. You could have stayed with us."

"No. I didn't want to believe him at first. I—it wasn't confirmed until midnight, and by then Neil was on his way here."

"But surely they've..." Cassie paused. "No, they haven't found him yet, have they?"

Ginnie shook her head.

"What are you going to do?"

"I don't know what we *can* do, Cassie. Except wait."

"I'm so sorry. But at least you have Neil with you. It's not as though you're waiting this out alone. But what a rotten thing to happen on Christmas."

"What a rotten thing to happen any time," Ginnie said. "Now, can we talk about something else, like what secret ingredient you put in your fantastic cornbread dressing or my recipe for Gran's sweet potatoes, please?"

"Sure." Cassie smiled tentatively. "But since I already know the recipe for my dressing, let's start with your grandmother's sweet potatoes."

Several minutes later, when silence filled the house, Ginnie looked up in surprise. The three men walked into the kitchen.

"I didn't think this house could smell any better than it did earlier," Frank said, "but I've been wrong about other things, too. Is there going to be time for us to go outside for a while, before dinner?"

"I think so," Cassie said. "But don't be too long. Remember Father McIntyre's appointment tonight."

"Oh, I'm sorry, Cassandra," the priest said. "I should have told you immediately. That's what the parish secretary's call was about. My evening appointment has canceled on me because of the weather. I hope this hasn't inconvenienced you."

"Ginnie, can you come outside, too?" Paul, Cassie's youngest, spoke from the doorway. "I want you to see the snowman. He's got real coal for his eyes. Just like Frosty."

"I saw him on the way up, Paul," she told him, smiling at his exuberance. "And he is magnificent. But right now I have to help your mother finish dinner."

"Oh, Ginnie, come on. It will only take a few minutes," the little boy said.

"Maybe later," she told him.

"Go on, Paul," Cassie prodded.

"Gee, Mom, it wouldn't—"

"Go on, Paul," Frank seconded.

The other boys, Mark and James, needed no such prodding. They were already in their coats and headed for the back door.

All six, men and boys, were clearly visible through the dining-room windows as they walked to the snowman, as was Flori, the mother of Ginnie's pup, who seemed pathetically hungry for attention.

The men nodded and pointed, obviously approving the craftsmanship of the snowman, and it looked as though Frank was explaining the engineering behind the construction, until Mark, the middle son, scooped up a handful of snow and stuffed it down the back of his older brother's jacket. James, of course, had to retaliate. And Paul could not be left out.

While the three boys scuffled, the men moved toward the edge of the woods, walking slowly but carrying on an animated conversation. A loud wail came from one of the boys, probably Paul, Ginnie thought. The three men turned toward the driveway. Frank came back on a run, breaking up the overeager donnybrook, but he waved to Neil and Father McIntyre, signaling them to go on without him, and the two of them, smiling, turned and walked into the woods.

Cassie, apparently convinced now that none of her boys were seriously injured, began counting out plates and silverware.

"You never told me how handsome he is," she said, reaching upward for still one more plate.

"No, I suppose I didn't."

"In fact, you never told me very much about him at all."

"No," Ginnie admitted. "I suppose I didn't."

She reached for the stack of dishes. "Here. I'll set the table."

How could she have told anyone about Neil without explaining how she felt about him? And if she tried to do that, she'd either have to lie to her friend or admit to herself that time hadn't healed anything, that she still loved him as much as the day she'd left their house in the country. She put down the plates and leaned both hands on the table. *Even more,* if that was possible.

When the males returned, en masse, to the house, Ginnie and Cassie had the table set. The only remaining work was to carry the food from the kitchen to the dining room, which they did while the others engaged in a flurry of washing up and drying of melting snow.

They seated themselves around the large, round table, elongated now by the added leaves, with only a slight flutter of activity from the boys.

"Father, will you?"

"Of course, Frank," the priest said. Reverently, he made the sign of the cross and began the familiar introduction to prayer.

Ginnie glanced surreptitiously at Neil, seated beside her. This was her life now and although she knew Neil would only be in it for a short while, she couldn't help wondering what his reaction to it was. She didn't think that he would ever ridicule it, and she hoped that somehow he could draw as much peace from it as she usually did.

She felt Neil's small start of surprise as hands were joined around the table, and James, seated on his other side, reached for his. She smiled at him, reassuring him. He locked his fingers with hers, completing the circle.

She barely heard Father McIntyre's melodious voice giving thanks. Through lowered lids she studied the contrast of her small, pale hand in Neil's large, darker one.

"And be with your children, Virginia and Neil . . ." The words penetrated her consciousness. "And their son, Todd. Give them the wisdom to meet the challenges facing them, and the understanding to accept Your Will."

Slowly and carefully, Neil's strong, tanned fingers closed completely over hers. How did Father McIntyre know? Unless . . . ? She glanced up at Neil's face, only to find him watching hers. Wordlessly, she returned the pressure of his hand.

Ginnie barely tasted the meal. She accepted the compliments she and Cassie shared, but suddenly here, too, she was the outsider. Cassie and Frank had welcomed her into their family gathering, but she was not really family.

And Neil— She closed her eyes against the surge of pain. At one time, they might have had something like this together, but that had been destroyed long ago.

She heard Neil's comments to Frank, heard him answer questions from the boys, heard his easy interplay with Father McIntyre, his compliments to Cassie. They should have been in their own home, she thought, fighting that thought, with their own children around them, not guests in someone else's home, brought together only by tragedy.

She recognized the low rumble of Frank's voice and from the scattered words she picked up, she knew he was relating a story from the campus. She knew that it would be humorous. She knew that she ought to listen, but she could not force herself to concentrate on his words. When laughter erupted around the table, she joined in softly.

"Now," Cassie said, smothering back her laugh, "how about pie and coffee?"

"That's a marvelous idea, wife. You and Ginnie go on into the den and I will bring it to you. Father McIntyre? Neil? Would you join the ladies? Boys, kitchen detail."

"Ah, gee, Dad," James said. "It's Christmas. You mean we have to do KP?"

"The ladies prepared this feast for you. Don't you think it's a little unfair to expect them to have to clean up the mess, too? Come on, boys."

Ginnie had been shocked the first time she witnessed this division of labor, but by now she had grown accustomed to it. She had grown, in fact, to enjoy it, for herself as well as for her friend. She grinned at Neil, knowing the thoughts that must be passing through his mind and wondering what would have happened if she had ever approached him with the idea that perhaps the men in her household should clean up after themselves.

To her surprise, he pushed back his chair and stood up.

"Do you need an extra hand, Frank? I've gotten pretty good at KP myself."

"Thanks, no," Frank told him. "I'm just going to do a little bit of supervising and I'll be right on in."

The rest of the evening passed quickly. Noises from the electric-train set in a corner of the spacious den competed with Christmas carols from the stereo and laughter from the boys and even, Ginnie was surprised to discover, from herself and Neil.

She had to inspect each of Paul's presents and each of Mark's presents. James, who considered himself a little old for show-and-tell, didn't drag everything out, but there were a few things of which he was particularly proud, and he did put these on display.

Paul curled by her side with a new book while Cassie was out of the room. Ginnie helped him with the words that were just outside his vocabulary range. She watched Neil sprawled on the floor with Mark and James and an enormous pile of Lego, which slowly assumed the shape of some sort of alien space-landing craft.

She tried not to remember other Christmases together. She tried not to remember Neil on the floor playing with Todd and his new toys. She tried not to remember the aromas coming from her kitchen. She tried not to feel cheated.

Darkness crept into the room. The lights from the tree were no longer enough. Cassie lighted lamps around the pleasant room. Paul began nodding sleepily, the aftereffects of too much food and much too long a day. Ginnie saw Neil glance at his watch.

"We really should be going," she said softly.

Neil shot her a look of gratitude, and Cassie, for once, didn't argue about her leaving so early. Father McIntyre took Ginnie's hand in one of his slender ones, and Neil's in the other. "My prayers will be with the three of you."

Cassie hugged her friend, as did Frank, a little self-consciously, before shaking hands with Neil. "I've enjoyed this afternoon, in spite of the tragedy behind it," he told Neil. "If we can help in any way, let us know."

"Oops, wait a minute!" Cassie said, darting into the kitchen and reappearing with a loaded grocery bag. "You're not leaving me with all the leftovers."

"What do you mean?" Ginnie asked. "Why do you think I come out here, if not to get away from those."

"No fair." Cassie remained firm. "I wrapped them for the freezer. If you don't want them tonight, just stick them in there. They'll keep till the Fourth of July, if need be, but I'm not storing all that food in my house to tempt me into gaining another five pounds."

And then Ginnie and Neil were alone in the car, in the dark, once again silent.

"They're nice people," Neil said after long, uncomfortable minutes.

"Yes, they are," she answered, pretending to concentrate on the road.

"You're fond of them, aren't you?"

"Yes. I am."

Seconds stretched into minutes before he spoke again. "You interact very well . . . with the boys."

She felt a tugging at her heart and a tightness in the back of her throat. She heard no censure in his voice, but she dared not speculate whether he meant—you interact very well with their boys, why couldn't you have done so with mine? Or maybe, just maybe—you interact very well with their boys, why couldn't mine have done so with you?"

Neil insisted on entering the darkened house first, and on checking out each room, flipping on the lights as he went. When he was satisfied that the house was indeed empty, he carried the food into the kitchen for her. While she put it away, he made what she knew was a necessary telephone call.

She knew the answer by the expression on his face, but she had to ask anyway. "Is there any word?"

He shook his head. "More of the same. Which means more of nothing. For God's sake, he can't be that hard to find!"

Ginnie saw the raw pain in his eyes before he turned from her. "I'm going to take the dog outside," he said abruptly.

She nodded silently. The pressure in her throat had built steadily. Now she knew she would not be able to force words past it.

Shivering, she adjusted the thermostat, knowing that the temperature was only partially responsible for the chill she felt, and then stood in indecision, not knowing what to do next.

Neil had not mentioned staying, but she couldn't imagine him leaving at this time of the night. And yet if he stayed, how could she just casually point him toward the guest bedroom? She laughed, a choked little laugh.

Gran's lessons in etiquette hadn't covered anything like this. No one's lessons did. Maybe someday in this changing world, there would be a book, *How To React When Your Ex-Husband Stays Over For The Night.* Chapter 1—"How To Invite Your Ex-Husband To Stay Over For The Night." Chapter 2—"What Do You Do When You Want Him In Your Bed, Not The Guest Room?" Chapter 3—"How To Not Want Him."

A worthwhile project, she thought bitterly. Maybe that's what she could do with the sleepless nights that were sure to follow when he left—if she could bear the pain of researching it.

She heard Neil at the back door, stamping the snow from his feet and talking softly to the puppy. Sighing, she went to join him in the kitchen.

"It's been a long day," he said. "I don't see any sense in waiting up all night for something that might not happen."

She moistened her dry lips and nodded, agreeing silently, knowing that she would be awake at least half the night, anyway.

"You know that I'm staying here," he said.

She tried to swallow down the lump in her throat. Again she nodded.

"Damn it, Ginnie, you don't have to look like you're afraid I'm going to attack you at any minute. I'm not leaving you alone in this house tonight."

Fool, Ginnie, she berated herself. What had made her think she would have any decision to make. What had happened that morning between them had been a fluke, an accident.

"The bed in the guest room is made up," she told him. "But I'll have to get you an extra blanket."

Later that night, awake as she had known she would be, she thought of the truly difficult things she had done in her life—telling Neil she wanted a divorce, getting in her car and driving away from Pleasant Gap, and him, leaving him in the park with no more than a hug, and tonight, turning away as he began unbuttoning his shirt and walking from his room to hers with no more than a casually spoken good-night.

The wind shifted, howling around the house. Ginnie would have to find that branch tomorrow. It was scraping again, reminding her of the terror she had felt the night before. There was no terror now. Neil had erased that by walking into her house. But her terror had been replaced by an aching loneliness. Just knowing he was in the house was both comfort and torture.

The wind clipped a pine tree, moaning through it, and rattled at a window. She pulled the blanket more securely around her. Lord, she was cold. In the snug warmth of her home, she was cold. What was it like outside? Where was Todd tonight? He'd have no blanket to cover him, no central heating to flip on, no comfortable flannel sleepwear.

She shifted in the bed, burrowing against the pillow. Neil would be thinking those thoughts, too. How in God's name could he stand the waiting?

Chapter 10

The blare of the alarm clock penetrated Ginnie's warm cocoon of sleep. "All right, all right!" she muttered as she fought her way up from under the covers. "I'm coming. I hear you. Shut up already."

And mercifully, it did. Ginnie peered from beneath the blanket. Neil, already dressed, shaved and smiling at this ungodly hour, held a cup of coffee.

"I've been waiting for that foghorn of yours to go off for hours."

She scooted herself up against the curved metal columns of the headboard, drawing the sheet with her, chasing the cobwebs from her brain. Neil looked tired, as though he hadn't slept well, but not overly disturbed. Had there been word?

Her "Good morning" came out in a throaty rasp.

"It really is, you know," he said as he walked across the room. "I'm surprised you don't have booby traps in your path to the alarm clock."

No. There hadn't been word. He couldn't tease her like this if there had been.

"Oh, no," she murmured, yawning. "I want to make it hard enough to turn off the alarm for me to remember the trip, not to injure myself."

"Here." He handed her the coffee, and she accepted it gratefully.

"Scoot over."

She did, from long habit, never forgotten, and he sat on the edge of the bed.

"What do you have against morning, Ginnie?"

She glanced up at him from under a sweep of her unruly hair. She saw no criticism in his eyes and no disapproval, only a gentle teasing.

"Nothing," she said. "I love morning. It's just getting into it that I hate." She yawned again. "Mmm. This is good coffee."

"Don't sound so surprised."

"I did, didn't I?" she said apologetically. She had been. The coffee was excellent. But she wasn't nearly so surprised by Neil's skill at making coffee as she was by the fact that he was sitting on the edge of her bed, beside her, and they were once again sharing the intimacies of early-morning coffee. And it seemed the most natural thing in the world to be doing so.

"You didn't sleep very well last night," she said, looking at the dark shadows that ringed his eyes.

He shook his head. "Neither did you." His voice lowered to a tone she remembered all too well, a tone she'd thought never to hear again. "Maybe we should have kept each other company."

She felt the blood draining from her face and concentrated furiously on the coffee. "Don't tease me, Neil."

"I'm not teasing." He stopped abruptly, took the cup from her and placed it on the table. "Maybe I was," he said softly. "What I meant was, maybe we should have stayed awake together, after all, since we were obviously both awake. But I think what I wanted to know was— Never mind what I wanted to know. Oh, hell, Ginnie, what I wanted to know was if you missed me as . . . if. . ."

"You know, that's the strangest thing," she said gently.

"What is?"

"The way you lose all your renowned powers of oratory when you talk to me."

"I do, don't I?"

"Why is that, Neil?" she asked expectantly.

He leaned toward her, and when he spoke his voice was as husky as hers had been. "Why do you ask, Ginnie? Do you really want to know? Or are you only making conversation?"

Suddenly, she wasn't comfortable anymore. She was trapped in the satin depths of his eyes, caught in the past when her heart had responded to his, when her body had responded to his. Only this wasn't the past, this was now. Ginnie had spent years getting over those emotions, driving the ache from her, telling herself she didn't want him. Now here she was, responding to a need within her that denied the time that had passed, denied the hurt, denied the loneliness.

She shrank against the pillows, dragging her head back and forth. "I—I can't."

"You feel it, too, don't you?" he asked relentlessly.

"Please don't, Neil. Don't drag it up. Don't make us talk about it. It won't do any good, you know. Nothing has changed. Nothing can ever change."

"You still love me, Ginnie. That hasn't changed, either."

"No!" she cried, pushing up against the headboard, scooting away from him, as though removing herself from him physically could tear that invisible bond that held her forever bound to him.

"No. You can't do this to me again, Neil. It's Little Rock all over, and I won't let you—"

The expression in his eyes shuttered. "You won't let me what, Ginnie? Talk you into doing something that you don't really want to do, seduce you into staying with me because your body can't deny that you still care? No. I should have let you leave then. You really wanted to go, didn't you?

"Was that when it really ended for us, Ginnie? Were those first few months here in Pleasant Gap only an illusion? I thought at the time that they might have been—there was a quality about them that was never quite real. I hate clichés, but there's an old one that says if something seems too good to be true, it usually is."

Neil shook his head to clear his thoughts. "I had no right to say that, and I had no right to do this." He drew away from her. "We both know why I'm here, and this isn't the reason."

Her eyes were enormous in her small, pale face. Her hair spread out like a halo on the pillows. He saw a pulse beating erratically in her throat and the uneven rise and fall of her breasts beneath the sheet.

But wasn't that the reason? he thought. Couldn't he have seen to her safety just as well from Little Rock?

Was there any real reason for him to have come to Pleasant Gap if not to try one last time to bring her back into his life?

Don't be a fool, Neil, he raged silently. Ginnie had made her life without him. She was happier without him. If he persisted, if he made love to her now, *if she allowed it,* it wouldn't be because she really wanted him. If he brushed away her resistance, she would respond, but she'd hate him for it.

He turned away from her, because telling himself all those things would do no good if he continued to look at her, still tousled and flushed with sleep. And turning away did no good, because Ginnie's image remained in front of his eyes, the mattress remained soft beneath him, the blanket continued to brush his hands. He could hear her heart beating. Or was it his own? God, if he didn't get himself under control, he'd take her now and damn the consequences.

"I'll be in the kitchen," he said abruptly.

When she joined him later in the kitchen, the first thing Ginnie noticed was the contents of her wooden box spread over the table. Neil dropped the picture he was holding and shuffled it in with the others, but not before she saw that it was the one of them on the seawall in Galveston.

"I didn't know you had these," he said in a soft voice that betrayed no emotion.

"I..." She pretended to be absorbed with removing the basket from the coffeepot and pouring herself a fresh cup. "I didn't take many."

"That's not what I meant," he said. "They were yours for you to take as many of as you wanted. I just didn't think you'd want any. You were terribly unhappy, weren't you, Ginnie?"

"At times," she said, not willing or able to say more.

"You've done all right for yourself since we got out of your life and left you alone. Haven't you?"

The shock and then the pain of being served with unexpected divorce papers flooded over her. "Is that what you did, Neil? Got out of my life?" She couldn't keep the bitterness from her voice. "I always thought you got me out of yours."

"Maybe I tried," he admitted, putting the pictures back into the box. "Where did we go wrong, Ginnie? We could have had everything."

"I don't want to dissect our marriage now, Neil."

"Have you ever?" He took out the pictures, shuffled through them and once again drew out the one of them on the seawall. "Have you ever asked how we got from this point to where we are now?"

"Have you?"

He held the photograph carelessly, forgotten in one hand. "The first time was in Little Rock, when I sat alone in the dark with a bottle of scotch and your note. Do you know what it does to a man when his wife leaves him, Ginnie?"

He paused, but he wasn't waiting for an answer. He was dragging up old wounds. "It's like someone has twisted a knife in his gut. The first thing he's aware of, after the pain, is a sense of betrayal, a breach of faith that maybe never is healed—I don't know. Then, when he can think, *if* he can think, he begins to wonder, what could I have done that I didn't do? What did I do that I shouldn't have done?

"I knew you were having trouble with Todd, but I didn't know how much trouble, not how serious it really was. Looking back, I can see things that I let slide.

I couldn't read your mind, Ginnie. Maybe if you'd told me more about your problems with him sooner, or maybe if I'd listened to you more closely, instead of waiting until they erupted into full-scale war, I wouldn't have stayed so blind, but I can't promise you that. All I knew was that you were unhappy, that I had failed to make you happy.

"It's unreasonable, isn't it?" he asked. "No one person should have to be responsible for another's happiness, but I had taken that responsibility."

Neil sighed and shook his head. "Whether you expected it of me or not, somehow I had made it my duty to make you happy. And I had made it my duty to make my son happy. And I didn't succeed.

"What kind of failure was I, Ginnie, that I could not make my family happy?"

"Neil—"

"Other men could. I was intelligent, aggressive. I could sway a jury. I was charismatic, or so I'd been told. I could charm the voters. I could soothe internal problems at the office and with the election committee. I must be doing something wrong at home.

"Of course I knew that. I'd done something wrong with Todd since he was born. And that's part of it, but maybe it doesn't belong in this discussion. Maybe it does. The move to Pleasant Gap was to be the cure-all, Ginnie. I'd make everything up to you for your unhappiness. I'd make everything up to Todd for his unhappiness, for what his mother had done, for what I had allowed to be done. I twisted myself around until I didn't know me.

"For a while, it was all right. For a while, it was wonderful. But then it all started again, and I didn't know what to do. I began looking at what I had given up. I began missing what I had given up. I began resenting giving it up, because it looked as though the sacrifice had been futile. And I didn't want to give up any more.

"I didn't want to be forced into choosing between you and Todd."

"Neil, I never—"

"No. You never. You never said it to me. He never really said it to me. But it happened, didn't it? The day I walked into the kitchen and found you holding him away from you, with blood on your face and terror in your eyes. I could have killed him, Ginnie. I think I would have if he'd hurt you any worse than he had.

"I know you wondered why I didn't punish him more than I did, why I only sent him to his room. For God's sake, I was afraid to touch him! Afraid that if I did, I'd never be able to stop hitting him. At that moment, I think I could have turned my back on him and never spoken to him again."

She whimpered. It was the only sound she was capable of making.

Neil looked toward her, only bleakness in his eyes. "But that was before I found out how much trouble he was really in. How much he needed me. I'd let him down so many times before, Ginnie. Can you understand that? By not realizing how bad the situation was with his mother. By not fighting harder to get custody of him when Ann and I divorced. By not picking him up for visitation when I should have that weekend Ann killed herself and leaving Todd there to find her."

A mist of tears blurred Ginnie's vision. She knew she ought to stop him, but she could say nothing.

"By not listening to you when you first started telling me he had problems," Neil continued in his relentless self-recriminations. "By manufacturing all sorts of excuses for him in my mind. By being afraid to look at the truth. Because the truth hurt too much. The truth led to some damning, illogical conclusions."

She heard his slow escape of breath before he went on in the same low voice. "My father's depression could have been a fluke, like lightning, something that strikes once. But if I admitted his problems, and then I admitted my son had problems, and I admitted I was unable to cope with his problems, where did that leave me, Ginnie? Except squarely in the middle—a link between the two of them."

He glanced up at her. "I said they were illogical. But illogical or not, those were the conclusions I drew."

"Why didn't you say something to me before now, Neil?"

"And destroy my image even more? When you're trying so hard to play God, it's difficult to admit any kind of failure. And besides, I wasn't really sure how you'd react to being married to a mere man. I always felt that you expected me to be larger than life, stronger than any man could possibly be, wiser than any man could possibly be.

"I'm not," he said. "I'm just a man. I'm not sure I wanted to believe it then. It took me a long time to accept it. But it's a lot easier not having to be God."

"I didn't ask that of you, Neil. I had no idea you felt that way. It wasn't necessary. Do you know what it would have meant to me if once, just once, you'd held your hand out to me and said, 'I need your help.'"

"Someone trying to be everything to everyone can't afford that luxury. Think back, Ginnie. Did you ever reach out for my help? Really? It took years and a major crisis for you to tell me something that had hurt you our first day home after our honeymoon. And when you told me that, you weren't asking for help, you were demanding it.

"Maybe you didn't realize the difference—I didn't at the time—but if you had asked me for help, we might have been able to talk through it. We might have been able to come up with an answer. Instead, you threw it at me—'here's another crisis, Neil. You fix it,' and I either had to fix it or disregard it. And at that time, there were so many crises going on I had to convince myself that some of them must be imaginary."

"I'm sorry," Ginnie said, recognizing how ineffectual those two words were. "There ought to have been something within me that told me."

Her heart went out to Neil, forlorn as he was, sitting listlessly in the kitchen chair, the picture of them forgotten in his hand. "But perhaps I wouldn't have heard it," she admitted, "even if it had. I had my own role to play, too."

Neil glanced sharply at her.

"I would never have forced you into a choice between me and Todd, Neil."

"I know that now. You would never have done that to me."

"No," she corrected him. "I would never have done that to *me*. You were always larger than life, charismatic and successful and intelligent and aggressive. I'd never have forced a choice between me and your son, because I always knew what your choice would be.

"I was never quite sure why you married me—"

"My God, Ginnie—"

''No.'' Her hurt bled through into her words. ''No. You've been honest. It's time for me to be honest, too.

''I think I was always afraid I'd wake up someday to find you'd realized you'd made a horrible mistake in marrying me. I had nothing to offer you. I wasn't as beautiful as the women you saw every day. I wasn't as accomplished as those you worked with. I wasn't even doing a very good job of making a home for you.

''I couldn't go running to you with everything Todd said that hurt me, everything he did that concerned me. I was supposed to be making a home for you where you could be comfortable and relaxed and away from the pressures of the world, not dumping more pressures into your lap every time you walked in the door. Lord, if I couldn't at least do that, of what use was I? I wasn't helping you in your career. I didn't have any great social contacts for you.

''No, I would never have forced you to make a choice between me and Todd. I had to take care of the problems all by myself. And I knew that if I worked hard enough at it, I'd find a way. I'd do it. And everything would be wonderful. And you would love me.''

''Ginnie. Oh, Ginnie,'' he said on a soft moan.

Through the silence hanging between them, they both distinctly heard the sharp rap of knuckles on the kitchen door. Neil swiveled toward the sound, and Ginnie half turned, her forgotten coffee cup still in her hand, but neither moved to answer the summons.

The knock sounded again.

Neil rose carefully from his chair and glanced at her. She nodded hesitantly. Cautiously, he slid the bolt, opened the door only far enough to see who was outside and then opened it wide.

A young couple, jeans-clad and wearing matching sweatshirts and letter jackets, stood there laughing at something one had obviously just said. Their smiles faded when they saw the unknown man at the door. Ginnie hurried to Neil's side.

"Uh . . . Miz K," the girl said. "Ah—is this a bad time? You did say the day after Christmas?"

Her timing was atrocious, but Ginnie had promised. "Yes, Debby, I did say the day after Christmas."

Ginnie motioned vaguely toward the couple. "Neil, this is Debby White, student editor of the paper this year, and Ron Hobart." She grinned. "Debby's constant companion. This is—" She paused. How did she introduce Neil?

Neil solved that problem for her. "Neil Kendrick," he said. "It's nice to meet you, Debby, Ron."

"Come on in," Ginnie told the couple, breaking the awkward silence that followed Neil's words. She reached for the folder in Debby's hand. "Do you have the manuscript ready?"

"Yes, but if this is a bad time, I can come back."

Maybe Debby's timing wasn't so bad, after all. This, Ginnie could cope with. An extension of the interrupted discussion, she couldn't.

"Debby has a story almost ready to submit to *Seventeen* magazine," she said to Neil. "I promised her I'd go over it with her today."

When they reached the table, Ginnie hastily stuffed the Polaroid snapshot back into the box and closed the lid.

"Do you want me to put that away?" Neil asked. "I have a feeling I need to make myself scarce, anyway."

Ginnie smiled gratefully at him and handed him the box.

"Me, too, Mr. Kendrick," Ron added. "I don't get to sit in on the criticism sessions. They usually send me to the stereo while they're talking."

Neil quirked an eyebrow at Ginnie but managed to smile at the boy. "Don't you find that a little dull?"

"Not really. Miz K's got some old stuff that we have a little trouble with, but she's got some pretty neat new CDs, too. We're teaching her."

"This, I've got to see," Neil said.

"Oh, well, sure—" The boy seemed suddenly to realize that he was talking to a stranger, a stranger who might question his casual use of Ginnie's house. "Uh . . . if that's okay, Miz K?"

Ginnie heard more than one question in his voice. Maybe she ought to explain, but what could she say? She decided the situation was too complex to go into at this point. They'd just have to accept each other.

"Sure. Go on," she said. "This won't take but a few minutes."

A short time later, she heard the sounds of a mellow rock beat coming from the living room, played at the top of the volume range she had established as acceptable.

She pulled out a chair, sat down and opened the folder. It took a few moments for her to be able to concentrate on the neatly typed manuscript before her.

Should she have sent the kids away? Would Neil understand there were things unrelated to him or to Todd that she had to do? How would he react to being cooped up in her living room with an unknown

young man? Would he think she didn't care about
Todd or about his feelings?

Neil had dropped everything to come running up
here. Did he expect her to drop everything also while
they waited? Well, she couldn't. She'd put her life in
limbo the years she'd been married to him. Oh, Lord,
she had done that. She'd turned her life over to him.
Had she expected him to provide her with happiness
the way he'd thought?

A niggling little voice in the back of her mind whispered to her, "Of course you did. You not only expected it, you demanded it." But another argued,
"Not you, Ginnie. You wouldn't be that selfish."

"Miz K?"

Ginnie looked up from the unseen pages in her hand
to the girl seated across from her. Debby glowed with
health. Intelligence sparkled from her deep-set blue
eyes. An almost model student, except when she
wasn't, Ginnie thought and smothered an unbidden
grin.

"We can come back if this is a bad time, honest."

"Nonsense," Ginnie told her. "I know you want to
get this finished." She also knew that she could put
Debby off if she had to, but it seemed unfair to. She
concentrated on the manuscript.

"You've firmed up your opening," she said.
"That's much better. You got into the story a lot more
quickly this time, and I think you'll find it's stronger."
She skimmed the rest of the pages. "Okay, good.
You've tied in your title. Hand me a pencil." Quickly
she underlined one word.

"Typo?" Debby asked.

"I'll let you blame it on that," Ginnie told her. "I
think it's spelling, though."

"That's just great," Debby said. "I've proofread that thing four times."

"Ssh," Ginnie said, trying not to laugh. "I'm reading." She leaned back in the chair, lost in the story. Debby could write. Ginnie had no doubt about that. And it looked as though fiction might be her strong point. She stacked the pages carefully and handed them to Debby.

"Well?" the girl asked.

"Well, when you correct that one—typing error, I think the manuscript will be ready to mail."

"Do you mean it?" Debby asked. "Do you really mean it? Do you think it's good enough to send in?"

"Not only do I think it's good enough to submit, Debby, I think it's good enough for them to buy. But there are no guarantees. What you need to do now is get busy on another story, because it's going to be at least two months before you hear anything about this one. And you want something else in the mail, so that if this story does get rejected, all your hopes won't be smashed."

"Ah, gee, Miz K. Thank you."

"Debby?"

"Yes?" The girl looked at her expectantly.

"Don't get upset if it's rejected. This is a good piece of work, but you've picked a really tough market."

"I won't," Debby promised. "Now let me tell Ron. He's convinced that he's going to have to wait the whole Christmas vacation for me to finish this thing."

"Miz K?" Neil asked as they stood at the front door watching the two young people scuffling through the snow on their way down the driveway.

"Yes." Ginnie grinned sheepishly. The idiotic name the kids had attached to her had always pleased her, until now, but it sounded strangely unfamiliar on Neil's lips.

"I like it," he said, and his voice carried a trace of a smile. "Just the right amount of formality for someone as venerable and respected as your teacher, and yet admired and enjoyed as a friend."

"You understand," she said thankfully. "They try not to come out with that name too often around other faculty members, but every once in a while it slips out. I hope you didn't mind this intrusion, Neil." She felt it necessary to warn him. "There may be more. A lot of the kids have adopted this place almost as a second home."

"Do you mind the intrusions, Ginnie?"

"No. Usually I don't. Usually I enjoy them."

"I know," he told her. "Ron filled me in on the story of the annual tree-cutting and tree-trimming parties and the Thanksgiving dinner you have each year for the students who can't get home for the holiday. You've built quite a family for yourself, haven't you?"

She tried to smile but couldn't quite make her facial muscles work. "I've tried."

Neil draped his arm over her shoulder. With only the slightest amount of pressure, he started to pull her close. But he released her. "I think you always tried, Ginnie."

By afternoon the sun had melted most of the snow. A few patches clung tenaciously to the dead grass in Ginnie's yard, but on the streets, what remained bore no resemblance to the pristine whiteness of the day before.

Cassie called that afternoon to report that her road was impassable and to ask how Ginnie was. How was she? Ginnie wondered. "Fine," she assured her friend, almost choking on the words. "Just fine."

Late that afternoon, a high cloud cover began moving into the valley, hanging threateningly over it and dropping the temperatures.

That night she lay alone and sleepless in her bed, listening to the wind howling around the house, listening to the branch, forgotten again until that moment, scraping against the window.

Her eyes were heavy with the pressure of unshed tears, and her throat ached from that same pressure. From the talking they had done, she convinced herself. That had to be the reason for this renewal of a grief she could no longer deal with. Not a dissection, no. They hadn't again reached the honesty they had that morning, but they had talked their way through the years of their marriage—a chronological narrative, bordering on the brink of confession, bordering on the brink of honesty, but not quite reaching either.

Ginnie told herself that she hadn't been more open with Neil because she didn't want to cause him any more pain than he already felt. But deep within her, she knew that wasn't completely true.

In those moments just before sleep, the real reason shimmered through her thoughts as clearly as the sun had glinted on fresh snow. She whimpered and pulled the other pillow close to her, burrowing her face against it.

Todd, she thought. Alone in still another freezing night. Oh, God, where was he tonight? Lost? Yes, of course, but where? And when? Was he all right? Please let him be found. Please let him be safe. Please let us know that nothing worse had happened to him.

And why was she holding this pillow? Neil was alone, too. Maybe more alone than any of them. She ought to be in his arms, taking comfort from him, giving comfort to him....

Chapter 11

Another breakfast. Quiet. Restrained. This time, Neil did open the newspaper and hide behind it. This time, Ginnie took part of the paper and hid behind it herself.

Neil had not brought her coffee this morning. Ginnie recognized the wisdom of his not having done so, just as she recognized her irrationality in wishing that he had.

Almost as if by unspoken agreement, neither mentioned the past. Perhaps, Ginnie thought, because they had both said so much the day before and yet hadn't really said anything of importance after the kids had arrived.

The blare of Neil's car horn penetrated their silence. They both glanced up, alarmed.

"Is your telephone out again?" he asked bluntly.

Ginnie lifted the receiver. The dial tone hummed steadily.

"No."

"Damn!" he muttered. "We're going to have the whole neighborhood over here because of that thing."

He took off on a run for the front door. When he returned several minutes later, his expression gave her no clue as to the substance of the conversation.

"Was that—"

"No." Just that. No. "I disconnected the telephone from the horn while I was out there. At least we won't have your neighbors calling over wanting to know what's happening every time the phone rings now."

"But—"

He poured another cup of coffee and stood at the counter, head thrown back, easing the tightness in his neck with one hand.

"That was Carole Flannagan," he said finally. "I gave her your number in case she needs to reach me again. I hope you don't mind."

"No, of course not." *Of course not?* Why would Carole need it?

"You remember Carole, don't you?" he asked. "It was her brother Mickey—"

"Who was killed?" Ginnie asked.

"Yes. This has hit her pretty hard." Neil gripped his cup with both hands, drumming his fingers idly along the side of it. "I guess we all have to work through these things in different ways. I guess Carole can't help drawing parallels between Todd and Mickey, can't help reliving her own guilt."

Carole Flannagan, Ginnie thought. Neil had only mentioned her once before, and that had been years ago. The parallels were there, she knew, but how had Carole known? *Idiot!* she ranted at herself. What had she expect him to do after the divorce? Go into limbo? She hadn't. She had a life of her own. Hadn't she expected him to have one, too? And yet the thought of his knowing people she didn't know, doing things she knew nothing about, seeing women—*You're not married anymore!* she told herself firmly. He had a right to a life of his own. Even if it meant there were other women in that life.

"I guess I just didn't realize she was still in Little Rock," Ginnie said calmly.

"She hasn't been back long," Neil told her. "She came back to help her mother with the business after her father passed away. I'm not sure it was a wise move. She's never been certain that if she had acted differently, Mickey might still be alive. And living in Little Rock has dragged up all those memories. And now, with Todd missing—I'm not sure she's going to be able to hold together. But," he said, putting his cup on the counter, "she's basically strong. She's going to have to be with what we're letting ourselves in for."

Letting themselves in for? Oh, God. Was he...? He *couldn't* be thinking of marrying Carole. If he was, Ginnie didn't want to know it. She didn't want to face it. Not yet. Not now. Too much was going on for that to happen, too. And yet, she couldn't leave the words hanging there between them.

"What... are you letting yourselves in for, Neil."

"Kids," he said. And a swift rush of nausea rose in her throat before he continued. "Disturbed kids. Angry kids. Hurt kids. And disturbed parents. Angry parents. Hurt parents."

Ginnie forced back the nausea. Not *his* kids, that much she realized. But whose?

"I don't understand. In your law practice?"

"No. I'm leaving that. At least for a while, until this gets off the ground. I'm sorry, Ginnie. I hadn't said anything about it, had I?"

"No." She shook her head. "You hadn't. You still haven't."

"It's something I've been working on for over a year, finding funding and personnel. It's like a parents'-action group for those with disturbed children or children who've run into trouble with the law, not necessarily just with narcotics.

"Only we'll be working with both the parents and their children, finding legal counsel and psychological or medical counseling when necessary, trying to stop things before they go as far as they did with Mickey or with Todd. We've put together a pretty good group of people, and we've gotten quite a bit of support from law enforcement and the courts."

"That's a wonderful idea," Ginnie said, stunned. "But what about you? Can you put yourself through the—the—"

"The agony of seeing other people going through what we went through?" he finished for her. "If I can stop it from going as far as our situation went, yes."

He saw the doubt in her eyes, doubt he had felt himself. Doubt he could no longer afford to let himself feel. "Damn it, I've got to do something, Ginnie. I've tried telling myself all along that what happened wasn't my fault, that I did the best I could, and I guess I really did. I did all I was capable of doing—at the time. But it wasn't enough. There's no way I can ever make it enough. There's also no way I can ever erase what happened. My only hope is that, somehow, I can stop it from happening to someone else."

"You're doing this because of guilt, Neil?" She had thought once it was his fault, thought the whole thing his fault. She'd moaned it time after time into her pillow, needing the solace of placing blame. But she knew even then that it hadn't been.

"Don't you think you've done enough out of guilt in your life?" she asked him. "Don't you think it's time for you to put that behind you? Isn't this just another example of trying to play God with other people's lives? You don't have to do that anymore, either. You've said so yourself."

"It isn't a guilt trip, Ginnie," he told her. "And I'm not playing God. I'm using my knowledge and my experience in an area where I think it's needed."

Ginnie felt her throat closing and the ache behind her eyes growing in intensity. God, was she going to spend the rest of her life crying? "You act as though there's no hope . . . for Todd. Ever."

"Is there?" Neil asked, and she knew from the tone of his voice that he didn't think there was. "Even if they find him this time and he's all right, even if they take him back to the sanitarium and find new medication for him, even if at some time in the future he stabilized enough so that it's safe to let him out with other people, is there really any hope for Todd?"

"There's always hope," she said, her words choking their way past her throat. "There's got to be hope, Neil."

The tears she could no longer control spilled forth. "Please," she said, sobbing, "Please. There's got to be hope."

Neil dragged her into his arms, cradling her to his chest. "Of course there's hope, Ginnie," he murmured against her hair. "I didn't mean it to sound the way it did. Shh. Of course there's hope."

At what point did his caress become more than comfort? More than reassurance? She never knew. One moment he was soothing her, calming her, and the next—it was not comfort she was aware of, but the lean hardness of his body against hers, the play of his fingers through her hair, the pressure of his hand across her back, the whisper of his breath across her forehead.

How long had it been since she'd been free to respond to the passion he never failed to bring to life in her? Too long, she knew. A lifetime.

Her breasts ached for the touch of his hand, her mouth for the hard pressure of his, her body for the completion it had been too long denied.

Her hands were caught between them, balled against his chest. She opened them, sliding them across his shirt, around to grip his back, as she turned her face to the opening at his throat—an unconscious movement, not planned—to the warm clean scent, to the taste of him that haunted her dreams. Her lips found his beating pulse as surely and as naturally as she found home each evening.

She felt his sharp intake of breath and the flutter in the pulse beneath her seeking mouth. He tightened his hold on her, almost imperceptibly, and she felt his lips moving over her cheek, tentatively, questioningly.

It wasn't enough. It would never be enough, she knew. Impatiently, hungrily, she turned her face to his, holding him closer by the pressure of her hands on his back, searching blindly for what no one but Neil had ever given her, that no one but Neil would ever give her.

His mouth crushed down on hers, not questioning and gentle now, but hard and hungry. The pressure of his hands bore into her, pulling her to him, and she went willingly as she opened to the thrusting possession of his tongue.

It had been too long, she thought, if the disjointed impressions of her mind could really be called thought. So many years of denying this hunger.

Her aching breast welcomed his hand as he cupped it. Not since the divorce—

She couldn't think about the divorce now, she *wouldn't* think about the divorce now, not with his mouth moving over hers, not with her soul singing in response. What was a divorce but a piece of paper? It ended nothing. She was still his wife, would always be his wife. Paper could never destroy what she felt for him. Just paper.

Paper he had asked for, she remembered with chilling clarity.

What was she doing throwing herself at him? Of course he was responding to her. But why? Not from any undying love. His emotions had to be in the same fire storm hers were because of Todd and all the raking up of their past. He was a healthy, virile man. She knew how to please him. He'd remember that, as they had remembered so many other things since he'd arrived in the middle of the storm. The responses were all there, their pattern had been set a long time before.

Ginnie moaned, dragging her mouth from his. She turned her cheek to his chest and leaned against him limply, unable yet to end the embrace completely, listening to the pounding of his heart, feeling her breath crying in her lungs. Whimpering, she loosed her hold on him and pushed away, trying not to see the puzzled questions in his eyes.

"I—I'm sorry," she said brokenly. "I never meant for that to happen."

"Ginnie—" With a touch as soft as his voice, he reached out to trace one finger along her cheek.

"No," she pleaded. "Don't." Oh, Lord, what had she almost done? She had to get away from him, get away from herself. She turned, stumbling as her legs almost refused to carry her away from him, and walked from the room.

He caught up with her at the front door as she fumbled with coat and purse and car keys. She faced him in embarrassed silence.

"Where do you think you're going?"

"Just…out," she said finally. "Maybe into town."

"You don't have to leave your own home to get away from me, Ginnie."

"No!" she cried. "No. That isn't it at all. I really do need to go—" She broke off, trapped in the quicksand of her own words.

"The streets are solid ice, Ginnie. You have no business being out there. It isn't safe."

"Not safe?" What was not safe for her was staying in this house with Neil one moment longer. "You forget," she said, hiding her turmoil, "I've been looking out for myself for a long time."

"No," he told her. "That's something I've never forgotten."

Angrily, he stuffed his hands into the pockets of his jeans. "If you insist on going out today, then I suppose I have to insist on going with you. And driving. I have enough to worry about without adding anything else to the list. Wait here while I get my coat."

* * *

Nothing remained of the beauty of Christmas Day, only frozen mounds of grime-smirched slush, as gray as the sky that lowered over them.

"Where to?" Neil asked as they approached the downtown area in his car, this time, not hers, and with him driving, this time, not her.

"Oh." Ginnie remembered that she had to have a reason for being out of the house. "The grocery store," she said. "Mr. Sims's, on the square." And then, remembering her overstocked pantry and refrigerator, she added much too quickly, "We're running low on a few things. Coffee and eggs and milk."

"All right, Ginnie. You don't have to explain why you want to go to the grocery store. Besides, I'm running low on a few things myself."

Mr. Sims looked up from the first of the two cash registers as they walked in. He smiled pleasantly at Ginnie, but when his eyes registered recognition of Neil, his pleasant features broke into a smile that transformed his usually colorless face.

"Neil Kendrick," he said with genuine and obvious delight. He wiped his hands on his spotless white butcher's apron and walked from behind the counter, extending his hand as he advanced. "I'd heard you were in town. Gee, it's good to see you. Are you going—" He glanced at Ginnie and back at Neil. "Good to have you back."

Neil gripped the man's hand. "Thanks. It's good to be back." But Ginnie noticed that he offered no explanation in spite of Mr. Sims's obvious curiosity.

She ducked past the two of them, after smiling her greeting to the grocer, pulled out a shopping cart, and pushed it down the aisle. Heard he was back, indeed.

Why hadn't she thought about that? Everyone in town would have heard he was back by now.

"I thought you told me you needed milk and eggs," Neil said close to her ear.

Her hands clenched on the shopping cart. "I do."

"You've passed them."

"Oh." Ginnie wheeled around and returned to the dairy counter. Neil watched her silently as she placed the items in the cart. "Eggs," she said. "And milk."

"And coffee," he reminded her.

"And coffee." Again she wheeled the cart around.

"Here. Let me push that for you. You don't seem to be doing so well."

"All right!" she whispered vehemently. "I don't really need any groceries. But you knew that already, didn't you?"

"Yes. And I don't really need anything, either. But we might as well pick up the things we said we were going to get while we're here."

A dozen eggs, a gallon of milk and a pound of coffee rattled forlornly in the shopping cart with Neil's shaving cream and razor blades up to the front of the store where Mr. Sims rang up each item and placed them, smiling blandly as he did so, in intimate closeness in the same bag.

Ginnie reached for her purse, but Neil shot her a glance that said clearly, *Don't you dare,* as he took out his wallet. She wouldn't dare. Not with that look in Neil's eyes, and not with the speculation she could feel emanating from Mr. Sims at the blatantly domestic assortment of items they had chosen.

Neil walked to the passenger side of his car, opened the back door and slid the grocery bag onto the seat. When Ginnie reached for the handle of her door, he shook his head. "Not yet. We're down here already. Humor me?"

Her senses caught at the elusive plea in his voice. Wordlessly, she nodded and let him take her hand and help her back up onto the high sidewalk.

The square was deserted now, not bustling with activity as it had been that first time, and yet it reminded her so poignantly of that visit.

"You still love this town, don't you, Ginnie?"

Did she? At first it had reminded her of something out of a dream. Then the dream had turned into a nightmare. Was what she felt for this town love? Or comfort, from a sense of habit? The promise she had first sensed in it was for a part of her life that no longer existed. "I think so."

Neil reached for her hand again and guided her around a patch of ice. "You called it Munchkinland," he reminded her. "From the Land of Oz. A magical community."

Yes. She had. And an imaginary one. She shook her head against the pain of memories.

"But that dates us," he said.

"Dates us?"

"Yes. It puts us firmly in the older generation."

"Does it?" she rattled on, anything, *anything* to keep from saying what mustn't be said. "You've got to keep up with these things, Neil."

"Oh, and if remembering a sixty-or-so-year-old movie doesn't date us, why doesn't it?"

She grinned then. Sometimes idiocy could be beneficial. "Television, VCRs, and a group of young people who have made *The Wizard of Oz* their latest cult hit. Didn't Ron clue you in on that yesterday, too?" Especially since it had been a comment of hers that had originally sparked Ron's and Debby's interest?

Neil chuckled. "No. He didn't tell me. He pretty well confined his conversation to rock music, basketball, and, of course, you."

What else had Ron said? He'd never been particularly discreet. Maybe she should have sent them away, or at least taken the boy off to one side and tried to explain the situation. No. No, it really wasn't any of his business. "I—I don't imagine he revealed too many deep, dark secrets."

"No. Not too many more than I've already mentioned. He did say he's in your youth group at church. They keep you pretty busy, don't they, Ginnie?"

"I suppose some people would look at it that way." She paused in front of the hardware store, staring distractedly at the assortment of garden tillers and lawn mowers inside. "I don't think of it that way, though. I enjoy having young people around me. I enjoy their exuberance, enjoy watching them grow. I enjoy having them like me."

"And they do."

"Yes," she said. "Isn't that the strangest thing? I thought for a long time there must be something wrong with me..." Her words trailed off. Here she was, admitting to him something she thought she'd never admit to anyone, something she had barely admitted to herself. "I thought there must be something terribly wrong with me because I was never able to reach Todd."

He squeezed her hand. "I wondered if you went through that, too."

"Too?" she asked.

"Too."

She studied their reflection in the window—both of them standing there so solemnly, to anyone watching just a couple looking at unneeded and out-of-season lawn-care equipment.

"You never asked why I went back to Little Rock."

Convulsively, her fingers clenched on his. "I couldn't bear to ask," she whispered.

He returned the pressure of her hand. "It was one more last-ditch effort, Ginnie. A concentrated effort to communicate with my son. I never did, you know. Not on anything important. By the time we left Pleasant Gap, I knew firsthand what you must have gone through, and I knew that even if it hadn't been for the—" He broke off and sighed. "Even if it hadn't been for the other, I couldn't ask you to come back into that hell."

A shudder ran through her at the thought of the *other* that not even Neil could bring himself to talk about.

"You're cold," he said, closing the door on his own memories. "Come on. Let's get some coffee."

They found the drugstore as deserted as the square. It seemed that only the two of them were willing to venture out on this bleak day.

Arlene Perks, who had worked in Johnson's Drugstore for thirty years, Ginnie now knew, looked up from her newspaper. "Hi, Ginnie," she said. "Hello, Neil. Saw your car Christmas Day. I was hoping you'd come in for a visit."

Ginnie went on ahead to the booth while Neil stopped at the counter for two cups of coffee, speaking briefly with Arlene, whose delighted laughter floated to the corner where Ginnie waited. Saw his car on Christmas Day, had she? she thought wryly. There was only one place Arlene could have seen Neil's car Christmas Day and that was her driveway. It was hard for Ginnie to believe that she and Neil had once sat in this booth in anonymity.

Ginnie smiled as he set her coffee on the table and settled his long length into the seat across from her. He shook his head, laughing softly. "Are you up on the local gossip, or do you want to be filled in?" he asked.

"I wouldn't laugh if I were you," she told him. "I'm sorry, Neil. I didn't think what this would do. You realize, of course, that everyone in town is going to know by tomorrow, if they don't already know, that you're..."

"That I'm staying at your house?"

She nodded.

"Does that bother you, Ginnie?"

"It shouldn't," she said. "But you're going back to Little Rock...soon, and I'm going to be left here to answer the questions—when you're coming back, if we'll continue to live in my house, when did we decide to reconcile?"

She could hear those questions now, unending, not malicious, but prying, all the same. And for some reason, those questions threatened to be harder to handle than questions about Todd would be should news of his escape leak into general knowledge.

Refusing to answer wouldn't help. The questions would still be there. And no matter how lightly she answered, each would prick, each would remind her of a loss as great now as it had been at the first.

She held her smile until her face ached, until she could no longer maintain the facade. "Look" she said, "I really don't want any coffee. Do you?"

"No," he told her. "Let's get out of here before the morning coffee-break crowd comes in."

Neil drove slowly through town, partly because of the ice on the roads, but partly, Ginnie could tell, because he was studying each familiar landmark. How was he seeing Pleasant Gap? she wondered. As they had that first day? And what was he looking for in this strange, silent journey?

They passed the small stone church. He slowed almost to a stop.

"What?" she prompted gently.

"The divorce," he said. "Does it give you—are you able to..." He remained completely silent for a moment.

Her participation in a religion so opposed to divorce must seem an anomaly to him. "It would only be a problem if I decided to remarry," she said in answer to his disjointed question. Which she would not do. At least not for a long time. Perhaps not ever. She knew that now.

"It wasn't a church wedding," he said finally. "You could—"

"Neil." She stopped him. She had to. "Don't."

He pulled to a stop a the edge of the park. A pilgrimage, Ginnie thought, to all the points of pain. No. All but one. Not even Neil would attempt the road to the farm in this weather.

Neil got out of the car and stood looking over the frozen landscape. Why not, she thought. Maybe together they could exorcise some ghosts. He looked up at the sound of her door opening. When she joined him at the front of the car, he nodded solemnly and together they walked into the park.

At their bench—*the* bench, she corrected herself angrily, she looked half-expectantly for the squirrel. He didn't appear. Neil also looked up into the tree. "I guess some things do change," he said flatly.

She dropped onto the bench. "I guess they do."

Neil didn't sit down. He leaned against the tree. "I didn't want to divorce you, Ginnie."

Her head jerked up, but after that one uncontrollable movement, she held herself erect, waiting, not wanting him to say anything else and knowing that if he didn't, she would scream at him to speak.

"But I couldn't go on the way we were," he continued, "sneaking around to meet you, to meet my own wife, and knowing that I might not ever be able to ask you to share a home with me again. I know now how sick Todd really was. I went through a period wondering if maybe I wasn't the sick one, allowing him to ruin three lives— No. Not him. Allowing three lives to be ruined."

She blinked hard against the tears forming in her eyes. She didn't look at him. She couldn't look at him.

"How do you untangle all the different things that run through your mind at a time like that?" he asked. "How do you separate what you thought then from what you learned later? Somewhere in that morass of confusion were fear and wounded pride and anger and frustration."

Oh, yes, she agreed silently. They were all there.

"You know what this town is like," he went on. "Every time I walked up on a conversation that stopped when I got there, I knew they were talking about the fact that you and I weren't living together. Every time I thought about bringing you home, I remembered that scene in the kitchen, and I knew I couldn't do that. God, I even thought about sending Todd off to boarding school, maybe a nice, strict military academy, but by then I think I was afraid to let him out of my sight.

"At some point, I decided the only thing to do was put as much distance between you and me as possible, and maybe then it wouldn't hurt so much. And maybe then each of us could get on with building a life. I don't think I really believed, when I first left, that it would be forever.

"But," he said, beating his fist against the tree, "I suppose it's worked out, after all. Hasn't it, Ginnie?" he asked in a voice so low and so subdued she barely recognized it as his.

One tear slid halfway down her cheek, freezing in its path. If Neil meant that each of them had been able to survive, then he was right. But if he meant that they were happy because of it—how could that be measured? Right now, all the things she had filled her life with, other people's children, other people's families, work, a house that was almost a home, seemed pale imitations of what they should have had.

"Yes," she said. "I suppose it has."

Chapter 12

Ginnie replayed the scene in the park through her mind later that night as she sat alone on the sofa. Neil had pushed himself away from the tree with no more than a terse, "Let's go." When they returned to the house, he had commandeered the kitchen table and the telephone and remained on the phone until late afternoon, talking to his office, talking to law enforcement officials, talking to Kirk. Talking. Now he was back on the phone and had been for over an hour.

A fire burned in the fireplace, imparting no warmth, imparting no cheer. Briefly, she considered plugging in the Christmas-tree lights, but it seemed that Christmas this year had never happened. She glanced idly at the tree. One package remained. She'd forgotten to take it to Frank, had forgotten all about it until just now.

She leaned back into the curve of the couch with her hand over her mouth. What a mockery, she thought, all the glitter and tinsel.

She was cold, in spite of the fire, in spite of the central heat. She thought briefly of going into the kitchen for a fresh cup of coffee but immediately discarded the idea. She had gone in earlier and unintentionally overheard part of Neil's conversation. He had been talking to Carole then, consoling her, Ginnie realized. Reassuring her. She didn't know who he was talking to now, but she didn't want to run the risk of learning it was Carole again.

The day had been hard on Neil. It showed in his face. It was drawn, haggard almost. It was as though the weight of the last few days had finally borne him down.

He brought two cups of coffee with him when he rejoined her in the living room. He handed her one, and she took it silently. After all, questions would prick at him, too. How many times could he bear to answer *nothing* when she asked if there was any word?

He prodded the fire and then restlessly paced the room, stopping finally at the mantel, setting his cup carefully on it, not looking at her.

"They tracked down the charges on the collect call you accepted."

She clenched her fingers around the cup. "Where— where was he?"

Neil gripped the ledge with both hands. "He called from a pay phone at a convenience store just off Interstate 40 at Morrilton."

"But that's—"

"Forty miles away," he said flatly. "On the other side of the mountains. He could have gone any direction from there, but tomorrow, when there's light, they'll begin searching the road north."

"It's been three days," she whispered. "They surely don't expect to find him—"

He whirled. "I don't know what they expect anymore. But you're right, Ginnie. It has been three days. If he were coming here, he would have been here by now. I don't think you have to be afraid of that anymore."

"I'm not," she said through her tight throat. She wasn't, at least not at this moment. "What I'm afraid of now is that he's *not* coming here. Where could he be, Neil?"

"God alone knows," he said. "In this weather, he could be—"

"No!" No, she would not let him say it. "You mustn't even think that," she whispered.

He ran his hand through his hair before sagging against the mantel. As she watched, she saw him swallow once and then visibly steel himself and straighten until he stood tall and strong in front of the fire.

"You're right," he told her. "If nothing else, Todd is resourceful. He's probably warm and dry right now. And oblivious to the worry he's causing other people."

He reached for his coffee cup, a mechanical motion, something to occupy his hands. He gripped it. "It's been a long day," he told her. "Why don't you go to bed?"

Was he dismissing her? It seemed so at first. Ginnie fought a quick flare of anger. She didn't want to be dismissed. But her resentment dissipated as she saw the signs of strain around his eyes and at his mouth.

"What about you?" she asked.

"I'll take the puppy outside and then I'll lock up the house. I won't be up late."

Reluctantly, she uncurled her legs and rose from the couch. She placed a tentative hand on his arm, but he stiffened at her touch. She dropped her hand to her side.

"You need your rest, too," she said softly.

He nodded, a quick, violent motion which spoke words unsaid. "Go to bed, Ginnie."

She filled the big, claw-footed tub in her bathroom with hot water, hoping to ease the tension that filled her, but in the silence of the night, each sound in the old house was amplified. She heard the back door open and close, the sharp, happy yip of the puppy and Neil's muted voice, footsteps, the grate of the fire screen being put into place, and later, through the old pipes, she heard the telltale sound that indicated water running somewhere in the house. The guest-room shower, she identified, when the noises didn't stop after a few moments. Neil was in the shower.

A wave of heat washed through her as she thought of him standing under the steamy spray, soaping himself, and then twisting with supple grace to let the water carry away the lather.

She moaned and jerked her eyes open to cancel out the image. So much for doing away with tension. The caress of the water against her skin had become more than she could bear. She blotted her body with the thirsty towel quickly, efficiently, no languorous drying; she knew instinctively that could only lead to imagined sensations.

She reached for her terry-cloth robe, belted it around her and applied single-minded concentration to the effort of brushing her teeth.

The old tub gurgled as the last of the water drained from it, and she could tell from the silence in the pipes that the shower no longer ran.

What was Neil doing now? She could not keep that thought from her mind. Brushing his teeth? Shaving? Toweling his body dry? Oh, Lord, why couldn't she keep her mind off him?

She pulled the pins from her hair, letting it fall around her shoulders and attacked it with the brush, but her mind refused to count the brush strokes.

She loved him. She had never stopped loving him. She would never stop loving him. She should have let him make love to her this morning.

No! her senses screamed. That would only take her back to day one—lost, hurt and frightened. She'd have to begin all over, erasing the memory of his lovemaking, erasing the memory of loving. She lay down the brush. She hadn't done very well at either.

With both hands flat on the vanity, Ginnie studied a steady drip from the sink. Neil wouldn't ask again, if asking was what he had really done. He wouldn't put himself in the position of being rejected again. He wouldn't put her in the position of having to reject him again. She watched her hand reach out, grip the faucet and tighten the handle until the drip stopped.

Compulsively, she draped her towel over the bar to dry, straightened her brush, put away her toothbrush and removed all signs of her use from the bathroom. She slipped into a clean flannel nightgown, high-necked and long-sleeved, unadorned but warm, and walked into her bedroom, where she slid between the covers without turning on a light.

A weak moon penetrated the cloud cover. Ginnie stared at it through the dappled sheer curtains, watching the play of clouds around it, listening to the branch she had forgotten, again, scraping against the house. It was the only sound she heard.

So she didn't have to be afraid anymore? That's what Neil had told her. And she wasn't, not of Todd arriving on her doorstep. Had that fear really disappeared? When? She'd lived with it so long, it had become a part of her. Could it have—was it possible it had just silently faded from her life? She knew herself well enough to know that she would be frightened if confronted by Todd, but she also knew now, accepted now, that *that* was something that might never happen.

She twisted in the bed, trying to get comfortable, and couldn't. But if she wasn't afraid of Todd, what was she afraid of?

She was afraid she would spend the rest of her life hopelessly loving a man who could never be hers.

Neil was doing well without her. Wasn't that where all their conversations had led? Maybe he hadn't wanted to divorce her, maybe he hadn't believed it would be forever, then, but he hadn't said one word about resuming their life together now, and she thanked God that he hadn't. That might have been too large a temptation to resist.

She knew, just as clearly as she knew that tomorrow she would cut off that blasted branch, that too much had happened for them to resume a life together. As much as she loved Neil, and even—improbable thought that it was—even if he loved her, there was no way they could erase what had happened. It would always hang between them.

She'd not been able to cope with marriage to him at the time they were married, she'd not been able to be what he needed. What made her think she could do so now? They would only wind up destroying any feeling they still had for each other.

Eventually, she knew, there would be accusations; there would be recriminations. How long could he go on being strong, assuring her that she had nothing to worry about?

And that's what he had done the past three days.

Ginnie saw that clearly, too. Now. He had been strong for her. He had been strong for Todd. He had even been strong for Carole Flannagan.

"Oh, Lord, Neil," she whispered into the night. "You've been strong for everyone else, but who's been strong for you?"

He was doing it again, wasn't he?

In spite of all he had said, he was shouldering the whole responsibility, standing up to it like some unfeeling monolith.

But he wasn't unfeeling, she knew. The signs were there in rare unguarded moments, in the pain in his eyes, the lines in his face, even the slump to his shoulders when he didn't know she was watching.

"You can't do it alone, Neil," she moaned into her pillow. "Ask for help. Please, just ask for help."

But he couldn't. She knew that, too. He had no one to turn to except, because of their shared memories, her.

Go to him, a voice in her mind whispered almost audibly. *He needs you. Even if he won't say it, he needs you.*

"No."

The sound of her own voice filled the silent room. Ginnie scrambled upright, piling the pillows behind her in bed.

Could she do that? she wondered—blatantly, leaving no doubt of her intention. Could she cross the darkened house and go to him? But if the thought of the pain of losing him again was unbearable, how could she live with the pain of rejection if he sent her away?

She could pretend to have heard a noise, she thought. She could put herself in a position for him to make the first overture.

"No!" she said aloud. "No, no, no, no, no, Ginnie. In this, at last, be honest."

She remembered the words, the expression in Neil's voice, or the lack of it, as he had told her, *They're trying to find out what's left of him. Is there any hope? I don't know what to think anymore.*

She had lain sleepless for only three nights because until now, in spite of herself, she had managed to put thoughts of Todd into the background.

But Neil had not been able to do that. He had been faced with them—*daily?* she wondered. For him, this must be the culmination of years of nightmares. And even though she had stopped him from saying it, she knew what he thought the search parties would be looking for along the highway north of Morrilton. How could anyone be expected to go through that alone?

She slipped from the bed. She would not let him be alone tonight.

And if he rejected her?

She wrapped a fist around the curved metal column of the footboard. He wouldn't, she vowed. He wouldn't.

In the back of her closet, in a zippered bag along with the coral silk dress and other relics from her life in Little Rock, hung a peach satin robe, still new in spite of its years. Ginnie shed her flannel nightgown and draped the robe around her.

At the back of her dresser, equally aged but also new from disuse, rested a bottle of perfume Neil had once given her. Her hand trembled as she drew the stopper from the bottle and lightly, very lightly so as not to overpower him with the freshly applied scent, she touched it to her body, remembering as though it were yesterday and yet also as though it were a half-forgotten dream, the pulse points from which the elusive scent would tantalize him.

Her hand faltered on the knob of her bedroom door. She couldn't do it, she thought one final time. She leaned her forehead against the door. Then she straightened, threw her head back and banished that thought from her mind. She opened the door and slipped through the silent house.

A fire still burned in the fireplace, protected by the screen, and casting its glow through the living room and into the dining room, where an etched mirror on the wall caught her image and threw it back at her—a pale wraith gliding though the night.

She paused in the hall outside Neil's door. It was open. Not, she knew, as an invitation, but so that he would be able to hear any strange sound in the house.

He lay on his side in the bed, facing the double windows from which the drapes had been drawn open, looking into the silvered darkness of the night and the darker shadows of the ancient privet hedge. She wondered if he saw that or still darker thoughts.

She slipped silently into the room and stood by the side of the bed, watching him, until something, the perfume perhaps, caught his senses and caused him to shift in the bed, to turn, to look toward her.

"Ginnie!" he whispered, instantly alert as he propped himself up. "What is it? Did you hear something?"

This was her last chance to back out. She knew it. She could make some excuse and leave the room. She barely heard the rising wind over the roaring of her own blood in her veins.

"No," she said. "I didn't hear anything."

She watched her hand, which had trembled so traitorously only moments before, as it reached without a tremor for the covers of his bed. She lifted them and slid in beside him.

She felt his start of surprise and saw it in his shadowed features, masked and yet curiously exposed by the moon's glow. He waited, barely breathing, dark carved alabaster against the luminescence of the stark white sheets. He would not make the first move, she realized, would not make it easy for her. But that was all right.

She wrapped her arms around his shoulders and leaned into him until his head rested against her breast. She couldn't tell him that she had come only to bring him comfort. His pride wouldn't tolerate that. And now that she held him against her, she wasn't at all sure that comforting him was truly the sole reason she had come.

"This is one sleepless night neither one of us needs to spend alone," she whispered.

"Oh, Ginnie," he moaned as his arms went around her, drawing her closer, as his face burrowed against her breast, as a long shudder ran through him.

They held each other, motionless, for countless moments. The initial movement was hers. She tangled the fingers of her hand through the rich darkness of his hair, pressing his head closer to her, urging him to follow her down into the softness of the pillows. As they slid downward, the hem of the satin robe caught at her knees, remaining there, baring her lower legs to the gentle abrasiveness of Neil's.

Flesh against flesh. The first touch of it jolted through her, much as a first drink of wine, before diffusing warmly through her body. Flesh against flesh.

She still cradled his head against her breast, but now he moved, nuzzling aside the satin, warm lips seeking equally warm flesh. She moaned and struggled closer. No other sound was necessary. Words might be needed later, but not now. Now—now she wanted no words to shatter these ethereal, impossible, wonderful sensations.

He moved as tentatively, as gently as she, almost as though he, too, were aware of the fragility of the moment. Carefully, with excruciating slowness, he slid one hand to her hip, content it seemed, just for now, to hold her.

She would not release his head. That, she could not do. But the sensations of the soft silk of his hair in her fingers and his warm lips on her breast were not enough. She freed her other hand and eased it down his back, feeling his smooth, firm muscles as her fingers inched lower, and lower, and lower.

She felt a small shock when she realized he wore nothing. He preferred to sleep that way, she knew but had not allowed herself to remember. He'd urged her early in their marriage to join him in bed unencumbered by night wear, but she had refused. She had been embarrassed, although she hadn't been able to admit it to him, to flaunt her body, feeling at the time there was something slightly immoral about it. But now she felt no embarrassment. Not with Neil. Nothing she shared with Neil could ever be immoral.

She freed her hand from his hair and moved her fingers across his shoulder in delicate tracery, down his side and around to his chest. Somehow knowing that she must do this, too, she found the small tie that held her robe together and unfastened it, drawing the satin with her as she slid her hand from between their bodies and moved against him.

Flesh against flesh. *Her* flesh against *his*. Ginnie sighed with the sheer joy of once again feeling that.

She had finally come to him. Neil's numbed senses took that in as he turned to her, drawing warmth from her, as his hands slid over the wisp of satin that was almost as familiar to his touch as her skin was. He wouldn't question why, now, she had sought him out when never before had she been able to make the first overture. Needing her was as much a part of him as breathing. He didn't think he could stand it if she pulled away from him again as she had that morning, and as she had the morning before.

He held himself in check until her warmth permeated him. Her gentle touch both soothed and enflamed him. *Ginnie,* he moaned silently. *Mean this. Oh, please, love, mean this.*

He felt her hand trailing fire across his back, to his chest, and puzzled at her slight fumbling motions until he felt the slide of satin being drawn from between

them and then the length of her soft, sweet self pressed
against him. His heart pounded against the wall of his
ribs.

Careful, he warned himself, knowing that if he fully
unleashed his need, he could drive her from him. He
touched his lips and tongue to the skin over her heart
and moved unerringly, moistly, cautiously, to the
waiting fullness of one small, proud breast. When he
reached the taut peak, he hesitated.

She moaned deep in her throat and pressed his head
to her as she insinuated herself against his body, moving her thigh into fiery contact with him.

"Slowly, love," she heard him whisper. "Slowly."

Then her breast was his, claimed as well as given, as
fires ignited through her body, fusing her to him.

He slid upward. His mouth found the pulse in her
throat and lingered there before moving up to the one
behind the shell of her ear. His hands slipped from the
satin, around, to stroke the softness of her with delib-
erate slowness.

Her mouth ached for his. She twisted beneath him,
but he still denied her that touch. His lips caressed her
eyes, her temples, her cheeks, and finally, oh finally,
her lips.

She sighed against his mouth as he claimed hers.
"Oh, yes," she murmured. She clenched her fingers
into the muscles of Neil's back as their kiss went on
forever—possessive, wistful, hungry, giving.

A tremor ran through Ginnie, and she felt the gathering of moisture behind her closed eyelids. How
could she ever have denied the…the rightness of this?
And how could she ever live with only the memory of
it? She forced back her tears. Now was not the time for
crying. Now was the time for loving. And if all that

remained after this night was a memory, then it would be a memory that neither of them would ever forget. A memory, perhaps, to replace some of the starker ones they had shared in the years before.

She felt Neil lifting her, easing the satin from her shoulders until nothing separated them. His hands and mouth moved with delicious thoroughness as they relearned her body. And hers, as hungry as his, refused to deny themselves the touch of him, the taste of him. He was hers. For this night at least. And she was his.

She felt him drawing her down, turning her, with his weight balanced over her. She caught his face in her hands and joined their mouths as he joined their bodies.

Oh, yes, the rightness, she thought in the moment of stillness that followed, and then she thought no more. She was caught with him in a warp of time stretching endlessly upward. Her body racked with tremors, but her soul sang, as together they sought and postponed, sought and postponed, and ultimately found that blindingly clear moment of unity which both shattered and bonded them.

Neil drew her head against his chest as he brushed the damp tendrils of hair from her forehead. Her cheek rested over his thudding heart. She caught his hand and placed it over her own heart. This was the language they needed now, she thought, not words. Not yet. She felt his arm tighten possessively around her as she sighed against him.

A noise, indistinguishable as it mingled with the sounds in her dream, awoke Ginnie later, much later, she thought, although she had no way of really knowing. The moon no longer cast its glow, but the darkness inside the room was greater than that outside.

She felt the tension in Neil's arm around her that told her he, too, was awake and listening. She heard the fierce pelting of moisture against the windows and then the howling of the wind. The wind. She knew now that was the sound that had awakened her. She felt the lessening tension in Neil that told her when he identified the noise.

They had shifted in their sleep. He lay on his back with her nestled in the crook of his arm. She traced her fingers to his heart and rested her hand there, feeling its even beat and the steady rise and fall of his chest. He caught her hand in his and pressed it against him as he turned to her.

His mouth sought her, his hands sought her, and she received him greedily, not trying to hide the desperation of her need.

When Ginnie awoke again, she was alone in the bed. Weak sunlight filtered through the windows and illuminated the tumbled bed covers and the two pillows crumpled closely together. No rain pelted against the windows, but a heavy drizzle hung in the sky. The sheets still bore the warmth of Neil's body. She struggled up from that warmth, running her hand wonderingly over his pillow before she piled the two pillows behind her.

The chill of the room touched her sleep-warmed skin, and she shivered and fumbled for her robe. Her foot brushed the coolness of satin, and she found it at the base of the bed, between the sheets.

She struggled into the robe and leaned back against the pillows just as Neil walked into the room. He had donned jeans and drawn a shirt over his arms, but it hung open. He sat on the side of the bed and handed her a cup of coffee, waiting until she had sipped from it before he spoke. He took the cup from her and set it on the nightstand.

"I'm sorry you woke up," he said. "I had plans of my own for awakening you."

She smiled and touched his cheek. Their closeness hadn't disappeared with the night. Maybe there was hope for them. Maybe... "Then I'm sorry I did, too," she said in a voice still thick with sleep.

He caught her hand and held it to his mouth, pressing a kiss into her palm. "Last night—"

"Shh." She wanted nothing to spoil the memory of their night together. "You know how hard it is for me to wake up," she said, and wondered at her brazenness. "I think I need some help or I may never get out of bed this morning."

Neil laughed and drew her to him. "You're right. You may never get out of this bed. Oh, Ginnie, do you know how long I've waited for this?"

She let her breath out long and slow against his throat. Yes. She knew. She had waited the same eternity he had. She slipped her hands beneath his shirt and urged him down to her, but he needed no urging. His mouth found hers, his hands parted the satin, and he sighed against her.

"You know," he said. His eyes locked with hers as with one finger he delicately traced her already throbbing breast.

They both heard the knock on the back door. Neil pulled away from her. Moaning in frustration, she began throwing off the covers.

"This is ridiculous," she muttered. "I don't mind the kids coming by, but they're getting earlier and earlier every day." She didn't stop to think as she jumped from the bed. "If that's Debby, I'll send her away, Neil."

"Ginnie. Wait," she heard him call out as she hurried to the kitchen. She was dimly aware of the compromising peach robe, but it made no difference now. She loved the kids, but surely they had seen the car in the driveway. Surely they knew she didn't need to be disturbed at this hour.

She flung open the back door without stopping to look through the curtain and stared up at the barely recognizable young man beyond the screen.

She stepped back and would have fallen had Neil's arm not closed around her waist, giving her the strength she so desperately needed.

"Hello, Todd," she heard him say.

Chapter 13

Taller. He was much taller, Ginnie thought from the safety of Neil's arm. Now she'd never be able to hold him off if he—

And bloated. Todd's features were a caricature of what they had once been. No clue remained of the intelligence that had once sparked from his eyes.

Ginnie's hand sought Neil's where it rested at her waist. His tension communicated to her as clearly as she knew hers must to him.

"Hi, Dad." Todd's voice sounded curiously child-like. "You're not mad at me, are you? I told Ginnie I might be a little late."

She felt the pressure of Neil's fingers against hers before he released her hand and stepped between her and his son.

"No, Todd. We're not angry. We've been worried," he said as he reached for the screen door.

Don't let him in! Ginnie caught her hand to her mouth to hold back her scream. They couldn't possibly protect themselves from this stranger who stood on her porch. Didn't Neil see that? She touched her hand to his arm, and he turned just slightly, so that she saw the pain in his eyes, and the plea. *Trust me,* he said without speaking. Could she. Did she dare?

"But I called," Todd complained.

Twelve years old, coming home for Christmas. Ginnie remembered Neil telling her that was possible. Oh, Lord. Was it? She forced herself not to shrink away from Todd as he shuffled into the kitchen.

"Hi, Ginnie." He looked around the cheerful room. "Wow, this is neat." Then he frowned. "Well, where's the turkey?"

She didn't know how Neil did it. From all appearances, he acted just as he would had he actually been talking to a twelve-year-old.

Was he? Or was this another of the malicious little acts Todd had perfected so early in his troubled life?

"It's in the refrigerator, Todd. Ginnie will have it on the table for us after a while."

"Great. Where's the tree?"

"It's in here, son. Come on."

She followed them to the living room, choking back a sob. How could Neil stand it? This boy should have been a carbon copy of him. How could he stand it?

Neil bent down and plugged in the tree lights.

"Oh, wow. Neat," Todd said, standing back to look up at the tree. "Oh, wow. That's the best one ever."

He dropped to his knees and fumbled beneath the tree for the one package that remained. He shook it. "For me?" he asked. And then he saw the basket, and the puppy in it, and crawled over to it.

The puppy whimpered as Todd picked him up, then snuggled him into his arms. Todd cradled the dog against his chest. "Oh, Charlie, oh, Charlie, oh, Charlie. I've missed you."

No. This was no act, malicious or otherwise. Ginnie turned away, fighting the sobs that threatened to tear from her, but not before she saw her own pain reflected and magnified in Neil's face.

"I tell you what, Todd," Neil said lightly. "Let me get my boots on and we'll take that dog outside and play with him for a while. Then we'll come back in and get you cleaned up. By that time, maybe Ginnie will have dinner on the table. Right, Ginnie?"

She forced herself to smile, forced herself to sound almost normal. "I'll bet I can do it by then. And afterward—" She calculated quickly. Todd was taller than Frank, but not as heavy. The sweater ought to fit him. "Afterward, you can open your package, Todd. Would you like that?"

"Oh, wow, yeah."

Neil brought his boots into the living room to put them on, not leaving her alone with his son, and she sent him her silent thanks for that. Then, reminding Todd of what they were going to do, Neil walked with him to the kitchen. Ginnie followed. Neil let Todd go out the door first and then looked back at her. And at the telephone.

Ginnie nodded her understanding. She waited until they had stepped off the porch to dial the number.

"Sheriff's office," she heard over the crackling in the line.

"This is Virginia Kendrick," she said quickly. "Todd is here."

"Are you all right, Mrs. Kendrick?"

"Yes. Yes, we're all . . . all right."

"We'll have a car right there."

"No! No, please." She knew instinctively that Neil would not deliberately lie to his son. "He's calm. I think we can handle him. We just wanted you to call off the search."

"Mrs. Kendrick, we've been looking for that boy for four nights. We can't just quit now."

"No." Her word sounded surprisingly like a whimper. Lord, what should she do? And how long would Todd remain calm?

"Please," she asked. "Can't you just—just give us some time with him? Just a little while? I promise, I'll call you back if . . . if there's any indication—" She broke off. Any indication of what? And waited, listening only to static as the deputy seemed to consider her request.

"A little while, ma'am. At least until I can clear it with someone else."

"Thank you," she said brokenly.

She replaced the receiver and leaned against the wall, running her fingers through her hair. She had lived in terror of Todd for years, and yet she had just begged the sheriff *not* to come for him? And what did she do now?

Christmas. Was that what Neil wanted to give his son? A Christmas Day. A Christmas dinner at—she glanced at the clock—at nine o'clock in the morning, for a boy who might be twelve for a lifetime or for an hour.

"Food," she said, for only by saying it aloud could she think of preparing it. She blessed Cassie for the leftovers as she snatched them from the freezer and began throwing them in containers, lighting the oven and the range-top burners.

She heard their footsteps on the porch and Todd's laughter—short, harsh, and yet somehow immature. He carried the puppy and only paused briefly as Neil brushed moisture from his hair.

"Why don't you put him back in his basket, Todd? Then I'll show you where the shower is and get you some dry clothes." He waited a moment after Todd left the room.

"They've given us a little time," Ginnie whispered.

He reached as though to touch her, then balled his fist and dropped it to his side. "Thank you."

Ginnie stared out the window after Neil left the kitchen. The drizzle had finally turned to rain, a cold, bleak, gray rain. How fitting, she thought, and then she once again snapped herself into action.

By the time Neil and Todd returned to the kitchen, Ginnie had managed to dress in jeans and a sweater, add logs to the fire, start the Christmas carols on the stereo and set the dining-room table. All that remained to be done was to transfer the waiting food into serving bowls.

Todd looked even more ungainly than ever dressed in a shirt of Neil's which was too large for him, and a pair of Neil's jeans which were too short, and Neil's black dress shoes. Neil carried Todd's clothes. She could tell by glancing at them that they were not fit to wash, but she motioned toward the laundry room, giving Todd even that pretense.

She began carrying dishes into the dining room. Todd seemed to notice her again. He reached for the bowl.

"Here. Let me help you."

She hesitated before handing it to him, but she did, and he took it.

"Where's your wedding ring?" Todd asked, and she thought this time she would scream. Or whimper. "Did you leave it on the sink again? Here. Let me find it for you."

"No, Todd, it's—" She glanced helplessly at Neil and saw his own sense of helplessness. Must they give him this lie, too? But she knew. Yes. This, too. "I think I must have left it in my bathroom. I'll go get it."

She closed her bedroom door and leaned against it. What fluke in Todd's poor, twisted brain had made him bring up the ring? Was he really remembering the times that she had left it on the sink? Or was he remembering the time he had taken it?

The box lay on her dresser where Neil had placed it two days before. With trembling hands, Ginnie opened it and snatched out the ring box. Dear God, how could she get through this?

She took the ring from its velvet bed, gave in to one long quivering breath and slid it on her finger, holding it in place as she looked at her hand, palm up, with the gold gleaming softly on her finger. She clasped her hands together, steeled herself and returned to the dining room.

Ginnie would never know how she got through that meal. She was acutely aware of Todd's monosyllabic response to any questions Neil or she asked. Finally, they pushed back their chairs and walked into the living room. It was time to open presents. But there was only one present. Dear God, she couldn't cry. She knew what Neil's cheerfulness cost him as he handed Todd the gaily wrapped package.

"Oh, wow, neat," Todd said when he lifted the sweater from the box.

Ginnie thought that if she heard *oh, wow, neat* one more time, she really would scream.

Todd shrugged into the sweater, as proud of it as if there had been six packages under the tree. With a sigh, he stretched out and hugged the puppy. "This has been the best Christmas ever," he said.

It had been a mistake to play Christmas carols. Ginnie knew that now as she listened to the words of "Silent Night." No. All was not calm. She crossed to the stereo and silenced it.

"What did you do that for?" Todd asked, sitting up.

"I thought—I thought I'd put on something a little livelier," she said, glancing toward the windows so she wouldn't have to look at him. Then her heart lurched painfully. There was a police car on the street below, and a uniformed officer approaching the house from each corner of her lot. "But if you like it, I'll play it again," she said quickly, resetting the tone arm on the vintage album.

Maybe she could stop the police at the door. What were they doing here?

Then the wind howled, and the branch she had never cut off scraped against the house.

"What was that?"

"Nothing, Todd. Just a branch," Ginnie told him, too fast.

Neil had bent to put another log on the fire. He threw it in place and turned to her, forming a silent question with his lips, but Todd had already scrambled to his feet, to the window.

She backed away from him, throwing a frightened, silent plea to Neil with her eyes. Of course there was no way he could stop Todd from seeing the police car, from seeing the officers.

Todd clenched the sheer curtain in his fist. "You did it again," he said, and Ginnie knew before he turned to her that he was no longer twelve.

"Todd." She heard Neil's voice, distant, because she was trapped in Todd's eyes, trapped with all the rage she could ever have imagined. She took one more step backward before he lunged at her, throwing up her hands to protect her face.

The blow never reached her. Neil caught it instead, stumbling to one side as it connected with his chest, before he wrapped his arms around his son, trying to restrain him.

Todd was unrestrainable.

He hit at his father and kicked at him, all the while yelling unintelligible words at the top of his voice. They tripped and went down, and Ginnie knew she screamed. She knew it because she heard it reverberating through the room just before she heard the splinter of wood and the crash of the front door being thrown against the wall behind it.

The two policemen pushed past her to the struggling bodies on the floor. She saw an arm raised, heard one sickening *thunk,* and the struggle ceased.

She ignored the officer's restraining arm and stepped forward. Neil, still on the floor, cradled an unconscious Todd to him.

"Are you all right, Mr. Kendrick?" one policeman asked.

Neil nodded, still holding Todd.

The officer reached for him, and Neil reluctantly released him. "Don't worry, Mr. Kendrick. When they get that bad, you can't hurt them."

"He's not a *them*." Neil's words grated harsh and raw in his throat. "He's my son."

The two men lifted Todd.

"I'm going with you," Neil told them, getting to his feet.

"I'm sorry, Mr. Kendrick, but I can't let you ride behind the screen with him, and we don't have any space in the front. You can follow us if you want."

"Will you be the ones taking him back to—back?" he asked.

"Yes, sir. We've already got the transportation orders cleared."

"Why?" Ginnie spoke for the first time. "Why did you come when you did? The deputy on the telephone said he'd give us some time."

"We did, ma'am. But when you folks didn't answer your telephone—"

"The rain," Ginnie murmured. "The line must be wet again. Oh, Lord, I didn't even think about that."

"And we couldn't raise you on the mobile phone," the deputy continued.

Ginnie glanced at Neil. He'd disconnected the horn because he'd depended on *her* telephone.

"The sheriff decided we'd better come up and check on you."

Neil walked with the deputies to their waiting patrol car and saw Todd, still unconscious, settled into the back seat, behind the metal grate meant to protect the driver, and locked inside.

Ginnie followed him but waited at a distance, watching him. He stood at the edge of the driveway until long after the police car had disappeared.

When she could stand watching his isolation no longer, she walked to his side and held out her hand for him. He stared down at it, silently, until she, too, glanced down. The gold of her wedding ring gleamed softly, a symbol of all that had happened—too much, she knew—too much—and of all that could never be. She turned from him and walked back into the house.

Now she was the one who watched Neil packing. There wasn't much. He laid out his things on the crumpled bed where only hours before they had lost themselves in an illusion. He worked calmly, methodically, until he had zipped up his shaving kit and zipped up his garment bag.

"Are you going to be all right?" he asked.

"Yes." She nodded. "Yes. I'm sorry."

"Don't be," he told her. "You did your best."

Had she? she wondered. And if so, why hadn't it been enough? Why hadn't it *ever* been enough?

"What will you do now?" she asked.

"What can I do? I'll follow them to the sanitarium, although I don't know what good I'll be able to do there. I'll go back to Little Rock. And on the second of January, I'll start a new job."

"Neil, I—"

He swore and threw the garment bag across the bed. "Ginnie—we could use your talent. We could use your understanding. We could use your knowledge of kids."

"You can't go through with that, Neil. Not after what happened today. Don't put yourself through this. Let other people take care of their own problems!"

"Like we did?"

She whirled from him and started from the room.

"Ginnie, I'm sorry!"

She paused for only a second. "So am I, Neil. Oh, God, so am I." Then she fled from the room.

Her kitchen. Her haven. Neil found her there, later.

"My things are in the car," he told her.

She nodded silently.

"How long are you going to hide in Pleasant Gap, Ginnie?"

She shot a startled glance at him. "I'm not hiding, Neil. I'm building a life for myself."

"Are you?" he asked. "Is that what you're really doing?"

"I have work here, Neil. I have friends. I have a—a family of sorts. I have a home."

"And you have a talent that's going to waste in this town. And while you have kids crawling all over you, there's not a single one you have to feel responsible for, is there?"

"That's not fair!" she said. "What do you want me to do? Do you want me to run back to Little Rock and tell everybody what a failure I've been? Well, I won't! If you want to go on a guilt trip, go ahead and do it, but don't try to take me on it with you. Don't drag me into it."

Neil beat his clenched fist on the table. "That's the second time you've said the words *guilt trip* to me. Well, let me tell you something, Ginnie. Yes, I feel guilty. Guilty as hell! But that's not why I'm doing this. I'm not going to wear sackcloth and ashes all my life because of it. If I didn't think I could do some good, I would *not* put myself in the position of feeling this kind of pain ever again.''

He sighed and forced his fists to open. "I don't like pain, Ginnie. I don't like the old wounds. I'd like to let them scar over so I can get on with living. But I'm not going to hide away and lick at them. I'm not going to suspend my life because of them. I, by God, am going to do something, and you have to do something, too. For your own sake!

"Ginnie—" He reached out to touch her, but she shrugged away from him.

"I'm doing what I have to do, Neil." She turned and walked to the kitchen window and watched the slow drip of rain through the bare branches of the trees in her backyard.

"I'm doing the only thing I know how to do... Now, would you please—" Her voice broke and her shoulders shook with sobs she still fought but could no longer contain. "Would you please let me try to get on with living?"

She stood staring out the window until long after she heard the front door close. She reached up to brush away tears and felt metal against her cheek. His ring. She still wore his ring.

She wrapped her left hand in her right one and held it until the ring bore into her fingers.

Then she sat at the kitchen table and no longer tried to stop the sobs that racked her body.

Chapter 14

Ginnie cut off the branch—broke it off, actually, with her bare hands. It was such a little thing, no thicker than one of her fingers, to have played such a major role in the events of the past few days.

She had the lock replaced and the front door repaired.

She threw away the remainder of the leftovers that Cassie had sent home with her. She thought she'd probably never want to see another turkey.

Though it was a ritual usually reserved for New Year's afternoon, she took the decorations off the Christmas tree and hauled the dying fir down to the curb where it would be picked up for the Twelfth Night bonfire.

And when she had done that, she placed the tattered remnants of Todd's clothing in their own separate garbage bag and buried them in the trash can beneath other packed bags of Christmas paper and litter.

She restored her house to order, but not her thoughts, and not her life.

The telephone-company repair crew finally arrived and replaced the housing covering the connection outside, assuring her that no longer would her line be vulnerable to moisture.

The kids began popping in again—first Debby with a new story idea, then Ron with a new record she "just had to hear," and then, it seemed, all of them, one at a time or in groups. And although none of them asked her, she knew that by now they, as well as the rest of the population of Pleasant Gap, had to have heard most of the details of the four-county manhunt and guessed the rest.

And eventually, Cassie's road was clear enough so that she could come to town. And she did ask. While they were seated at opposite ends of Ginnie's couch, each curled with a second cup of coffee. After Ginnie had talked about everything she could think of, except the happenings of the past week.

"What are you going to do now, Ginnie?"

"Do?" Cassie's question was reasonable, something Ginnie had asked herself countless times since Neil left. She leaned back, propping her elbow on the the couch cushion, and cradling her head in her open palm. "I don't suppose I'm going to do anything, Cassie. Except try to pick up from where I was Christmas Eve and go on."

"But can you do that?"

"I have to, don't I?"

"I don't know, Ginnie. Do you? Or do you only think that's what you have to do? When you love someone as much as you obviously love Neil—no, don't deny it—you ought to be able to find a way to be together."

"Oh, Cassie. We tried. Each of us tried."

"But did you try together?"

"No," Ginnie admitted. "I guess that's the one thing we never did."

"Well?"

"Well. It takes two to try together." She lifted her head and dropped her hand along the back of the sofa. "Not one. Not just me."

"Well?" Cassie persisted.

"Neil has made a new life for himself. That's obvious. And there's no place in it for me. Except on the very outskirts. He wants my help *professionally*, Cassie, not personally. He regretted that our marriage ended. He regretted the way our marriage ended. But that's it, you see. Past tense. It has ended."

"And is that the way you feel, Ginnie? That it's all past tense?"

"I don't think what I feel matters now," Ginnie said. "I survived losing him once. I'll survive this. What I couldn't survive is being around him every day and only being someone who used to mean something to him."

Ginnie's hand lay along the back of the sofa between them. Cassie reached over and clasped it. "What I think is that you've lost sight of something pretty important. The vows that you and Neil made to each other. Shared memories. Shared pain. Shared love. I know that you have to protect yourself, but are you absolutely sure that isn't what Neil is doing, too?"

"Cassie," she cried, "you weren't here. You can't know."

"No. I wasn't here. But I was at my house Christmas Day. And because you hadn't told me anything about him, I didn't have any preconceived notions. All I know about Neil Kendrick is what I saw that day, and he didn't act like a man who thought about you in the past tense."

"Maybe he didn't," Ginnie admitted, sighing. Oh, how she wished it were true. "But he certainly didn't act like a person who thought there was any future, either."

"Did you?" Cassie asked. "I'm sorry, Ginnie. I'm prying where I don't have any right to pry."

Ginnie smiled at her, a wan little smile. "I know you don't mean to hurt me, Cassie, but don't you think I've been over all this in my mind? Look, let me get us some more coffee and let's change the subject."

"No," Cassie said. "No, thanks. I hate to leave you now, but I really ought to get me and my groceries home. Are you going to be all right?"

"Of course I am," Ginnie told her.

"Will I see you at church tomorrow?"

What Ginnie needed now more than anything else was solitude, not the well-meaning questions that were sure to be asked by all her friends.

"No. I don't think so. I have two days before school starts. What I'd like to do is spend some time by myself, maybe even get away for a little while. Would you mind passing the word around to the kids that I really don't want company?"

"I'm not sure that will work," Cassie said, laughing, "but of course I'll do it. Do you need anything?"

"No," Ginnie told her. "Nothing except time."

* * *

Time. Time to heal. Time to forget. It had worked well for her once. But Ginnie had forgotten, until now, how much time it took to heal. How much time it took to forget.

She sat alone on New Year's Eve with only soft music, the glow from the fire and the sleeping puppy for company. When she heard the church bells and the fireworks and the few scattered shots at midnight, heralding the new year, she put the screen in front of the fire and went to bed.

Two days alone were a mistake. She admitted that long before they were over, but the hectic rush of starting back to school after break didn't seem to be much better.

"Damn you, Neil Kendrick," she cried one sleepless night, pounding her fist into the pillow. "Why didn't you stay out of my life? Why did you have to come here? I had everything just the way I wanted it before you came back. Now it's not," she moaned. "Now it's not."

Neil called her on Friday morning, six weeks later. He caught her between classes and devastated her with just the sound of his voice over the telephone line.

"I have to see you, Ginnie."

"I don't think that's a good idea, Neil," she managed to say.

"I'll be there this afternoon."

"No, Neil. Don't."

"This afternoon, Ginnie."

The rest of her classes passed in a blur. She put Debby in charge of the newsroom, got in her car shortly after lunch and then realized that she didn't know where to go.

Not home. Not yet.

Not just to sit and wait for Neil.

She had recognized the determination in his voice. She'd heard it too many times before to mistake it. But she didn't know the cause of it.

Was he coming to push her into joining him in that impossible venture of his? If so, the answer would be no. Painfully, finally, no. She could not do that to herself.

Or was he, as she had caught herself wondering in the middle of the night, wanting more from her than that?

She had tried. Lord, how she had tried to make their marriage work. It hadn't. She'd loved him then, and it hadn't been enough. And had anything really changed?

She found herself at the park. She set the brake on her Bronco and sat there looking over the barren landscape. How fitting, she thought grimly.

She pocketed her keys and climbed out of the car, shrugging into her coat as a harsh wind bit at her. It was February, and spring would be here soon. But it wasn't here yet. Not just yet.

Her legs carried her automatically—she could have found this path blindfolded—to a solitary bench beneath a still-bare oak.

She pulled her collar up around her face and stuffed her fists into her pockets as she sat on the bench. So much had happened to them at this very spot. So much promise. So much disillusionment. So much happiness. So much pain.

It will be wonderful, she had promised in the exuberance of youth. And she had tried. And he had tried.

But did you try together?

Had they?

And you, Ginnie, did you ever really reach out to me?

Had she?

She stared across the park, at a solitary tree. Soon, when the leaves budded out, she'd make a special trip to this park to find out what kind of tree that was. As much as she had stared at it, she ought to know what kind of tree it was.

She loosed one long, quavering breath. Too much had happened. Too much. For better or for worse, she had promised. And she had certainly seen *the worse.*

Why couldn't Neil have told her some of what he felt *then,* instead of waiting until it was too late? Why, after it was all over, did he show her a side of him that she had searched for, for years? God, she wanted to hate him. It would be so much easier if she hated him.

But what about forgiving him, Ginnie?

Forgive him? Even as the words whispered through her mind, she knew that anything she had not already forgiven Neil, she had when she watched him holding Todd unconscious in his lap.

It would be so much easier if she could blame Neil for all that had happened. If she could blame Todd for all that had happened. But she couldn't even take solace in that anymore.

If you can't blame Neil, and you can't blame Todd, who do you blame, Ginnie? If you've forgiven Neil, who have you not forgiven? Because it's in you still.

"Oh, God," she moaned. "I tried. I really tried."

"I thought I might find you here."

Ginnie jerked her head around at the sound of Neil's voice. He stood watching her for a moment, then slid onto the bench beside her. He was so solemn, she thought. She hadn't seen him laugh in years, except—except Christmas Day, with her, and that morning just before Todd came back.

What had happened to them? What in God's name had happened to them?

"I was trying to gather my courage," she admitted to him. "And to find some answers."

"Have you?" he asked.

"Neil..." Her voice broke. "Did I—could I have done things differently? Could I have stopped what happened?"

He put his arm over her shoulder. She felt that she ought to draw away from him, but she couldn't quite remember why.

"You're asking the same questions I asked myself," he said with incredible tenderness. "And the answer is, probably not. But maybe. Maybe we both could have."

A sob caught in her throat.

"If we had been different people. Or even if we had known what to do. But we weren't. And we didn't. Can you forgive me, Ginnie?"

"Forgive you?" she asked on a sob. "I have. I already have."

"Then," he said, drawing her to him, "what you have to do now is forgive yourself."

That was it. Oh, God, yes, that was it. The answer to the question she had only today been able to bring herself to ask.

"How?" she whispered. "How?"

He pressed her face to his chest, holding her against his warmth. "Each of us has to find our own way," he told her. "It's easier, much easier, to forgive someone else. I'd help you if I could. I'll be there for you if you'll let me be. But you are the only one who can do it."

She thought of the years of anguish, and of Todd playing with the collie puppy under the Christmas tree. Could she do that? Could she find a way?

"I have to," she moaned.

"Yes," he whispered, brushing her hair from her forehead, "you do. And you will."

He held her quiet and still in the warmth of his arms. "Ginnie," he said softly, "you asked me once why I lost my powers of speech around you, and I was afraid to tell you because I didn't know how you would react to my answer. I still don't know how you'll respond, but I have to tell you. Partly because of the things you said, but mostly because I need to say it."

She twisted to look up at him, but with gentle pressure he held her head down, her face against his chest.

"I'm told that at times I can be eloquent," he said, and she heard a wry humor in those words, a humor that quickly faded. "I don't know about that. I don't really care about that. But I do care about you. I've never been able to tell you what I really mean, Ginnie. Not in the important things. If I manage to say anything, it usually comes out twisted and garbled. The strangest thing happened to me the first time I saw you. I wanted you, then and forever, just like that. And I barely managed to ask you to have dinner with me."

He took a long, deep breath. "And when I left here over a month ago, I still wanted you—then and forever."

Her heart lurched painfully in her chest.

"But I couldn't say it. Instead, I got out some garbled words that must have sounded like a job offer. I love you, Ginnie. I've loved you since the day you first interviewed me. I don't know how to make you believe that. I have trouble speaking with you, only with you, because what you think and what you feel and what you answer is so important to me.

"I thought, after I came up here at Christmastime, that I was probably the biggest fool in the world because you had made a new life for yourself. There didn't seem to be any room for me in it. Until you came to me that night. You would never have done that if you didn't love me, too."

His arms tightened around her, almost as though he was afraid she'd move away. "And if I had thought the years since our divorce were hell, I found out these past weeks that I didn't know the meaning of the word.

"I went home and looked around my empty apartment, and I looked around my empty life, and then I looked ahead into the empty years to come. Ginnie, I don't want to spend those years without you."

She pushed away from him, and he let her go. There was a flurry in the tree above them, and a raucous squawking from the squirrel perched on a branch, swishing his tail in indignation.

"I've made you so many promises I haven't been able to keep," she said. "I'm afraid, Neil."

"Oh, God, love, so am I. I don't want to fail you again."

"Have we ever admitted that before?"

He shook his head. "I don't think so, Ginnie. I'm ashamed to admit this now, but I don't think I ever let myself be that honest."

"Neither did I," she whispered. "Neither did I."

"It won't be easy," he told her. "I'd be lying to both of us if I told you it would be. But we can do it, Ginnie. Together, we can do it. We've proved we can survive the worst."

He stood up. "You once told me that I had never reached out my hand to you and asked you for your help." He held his hand toward her. "Well, I'm doing it now. And I'm offering mine to you."

She looked at his hand, strong, tanned and capable, as he stretched it forth to her. Yes, she had said that. She had prayed for that. And now that he was doing it, did she have the strength she needed to reach out to him? That she would need to face the future with him?

Where is your faith, Ginnie?

She remembered their hands as they had been locked together during the prayer on Christmas Day. Maybe neither one of them was strong enough, alone. But together they would be. They had been tempered, and tried. Oh, yes. Together, they were.

She looked up into Neil's eyes. Clouded now. Waiting. A hesitant smile softened his features, and she felt her own answering smile, as hesitant as his.

Knowing that she had no other choice, that this was what she wanted above all else, and that this was what

Neil wanted above all else, Ginnie stretched out her slender hand to his.

She felt the strength in his clasp. She felt the strength in hers.

"Ah, Ginnie, we'll not be sorry," he promised.

She rose from the bench. Still holding his hand, she walked back into his arms and welcomed him back into her life.

* * * * *

Continuing in October from Silhouette Books...

This exciting new cross-line continuity series unites five of your favorite authors as they weave five connected novels about love, marriage—and Daddy's unexpected need for a baby carriage!

You loved

THE BABY NOTION by Dixie Browning
(Desire 7/96)

BABY IN A BASKET by Helen R. Myers
(Romance 8/96)

MARRIED...WITH TWINS! by Jennifer Mikels
(Special Edition 9/96)

And the romance in New Hope, Texas, continues with:

HOW TO HOOK A HUSBAND (AND A BABY)
by Carolyn Zane (Yours Truly 10/96)

She vowed to get hitched by her thirtieth birthday. But plain-Jane Wendy Wilcox didn't have a clue how to catch herself a husband—until Travis, her sexy neighbor, offered to teach her what a man really wants in a wife....

And look for the thrilling conclusion to the series in:

DISCOVERED: DADDY
by Marilyn Pappano (Intimate Moments 11/96)

DADDY KNOWS LAST continues each month...
only in V *Silhouette*®

Look us up on-line at: http://www.romance.net

DKL-YT

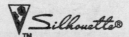

This October, be the first to read these wonderful authors as they make their dazzling debuts!

THE WEDDING KISS by Robin Wells
(Silhouette Romance #1185)
A reluctant bachelor rescues the woman he loves
from the man she's about to marry—and turns into
a willing groom himself!

THE SEX TEST by Patty Salier
(Silhouette Desire #1032)
A pretty professor learns there's more to making love
than meets the eye when she takes lessons from
a sexy stranger.

IN A FAMILY WAY by Julia Mozingo
(Special Edition #1062)
A woman without a past finds shelter in the arms of
a handsome rancher. Can she trust him to protect
her unborn child?

UNDER COVER OF THE NIGHT by Roberta Tobeck
(Intimate Moments #744)
A rugged government agent encounters the woman he has
always loved. But past secrets could threaten their future.

DATELESS IN DALLAS by Samantha Carter
(Yours Truly)
A hapless reporter investigates how to find the perfect
mate—and winds up falling for her handsome rival!

Don't miss the brightest stars of tomorrow!

Only from Silhouette®

FORTUNE'S Children™

Bestselling Author
BARBARA
BOSWELL

Continues the twelve-book series—FORTUNE'S CHILDREN—
in **October 1996** with Book Four

STAND-IN BRIDE

When Fortune Company executive Michael Fortune needed help
warding off female admirers after being named one of the ten most
eligible bachelors in the United States, he turned to his faithful
assistant, Julia Chandler. Julia agreed to a pretend engagement, but
what starts as a charade produces an unexpected Fortune heir....

MEET THE FORTUNES—a family whose legacy is greater than riches.
Because where there's a will...there's a *wedding!*

"Ms. Boswell is one of those rare treasures who combines humor
and romance into sheer magic."   —*Rave Reviews*

*A CASTING CALL TO
ALL FORTUNE'S CHILDREN FANS!*
If you are truly one of the fortunate
you may win a trip to
Los Angeles to audition for
Wheel of Fortune®. Look for
details in all retail Fortune's Children titles!

Look us up on-line at: http://www.romance.net   FC-4-C

There's nothing quite like a family

The new miniseries by
Pat Warren

Three siblings are about to be reunited.
And each finds love along the way....

HANNAH
Her life is about to change now that she's met
the irresistible Joel Merrick in HOME FOR HANNAH
(Special Edition #1048, August 1996).

MICHAEL
He's been on his own all his life. Now he's
going to take a risk on love...and
take part in the reunion he's been
waiting for in MICHAEL'S HOUSE
(Intimate Moments #737, September 1996).

KATE
A job as a nanny leads her to Aaron Carver,
his adorable baby daughter and the
fulfillment of her dreams in KEEPING KATE
(Special Edition #1060, October 1996).

Meet these three siblings from

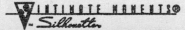

Silhouette SPECIAL EDITION®

and

V INTIMATE MOMENTS®
™ *Silhouette*

Look us up on-line at: http://www.romance.net

REUNION